COUNTDOWN T

COUNTDOWN TO ACTION!

JOAN MARIE VERBA

**FTL Publications
Minnetonka, Minnesota**

Countdown to Action copyright © 2008 by Joan Marie Verba
www.joanmarieverba.com

FTL Publications
P O Box 1363
Minnetonka, MN 55345-0363
www.ftlpublications.com
mail@ftlpublications.com

Cover art copyright © 2008 by Steve Kyte

Printed in the United States of America

ISBN 978-0-9653575-7-9

Thunderbirds ™ & © 1964, 1999 and 2008 ITC Entertainment Group Limited. 'Thunderbirds' is a Gerry Anderson Production. Licensed by Granada Ventures Ltd. All rights reserved.

For Daria

1

Dying in a Colorado wildfire was not what Jefferson Tracy, Air Force Academy class of 2031, had in mind to do that day. His orders, from the Air Force Academy commandant, at the Governor's request, were to deliver firefighters to the danger zone and to dump chemicals on the blaze. So here he was, flying in close formation with his roommate and fellow pilot, Timothy Casey, right through the smoke and heat. He could see Tim flying the other plane through his own cockpit window. The modern firefighting jets were slightly larger than a commuter jet, and they required expert pilots such as Jeff and Tim to handle them.

"Whew, that was close!" Tim called over the radio.

"Yeah, that flame rushed up like a geyser," Jeff replied. "I thought it would fry the plane for sure."

"Lucky for us we're the best pilots at the Academy," Tim said immodestly, though Jeff could almost see Tim wink as Jeff glanced to his left. "Evasive action is second nature."

"Well, we've delivered two dozen firefighters and dropped two loads of chemicals, so I guess it's time to get back to base," Jeff said.

"I bet we get back before the Colorado Air National Guard."

"That's easy, since they're so spread out. They wouldn't have called for Academy cadets if they weren't short-handed there."

"Still, I think we did as good a job as they do."

"We sure did!" Jeff said proudly.

They flew eastward, high out of reach of the flames. Jeff saw the wide firebreak ahead, cleared so that the flames would not reach inhabited areas. Scanning the ground near the deserted highway, Jeff radioed to Tim, "Say, Tim, I think I see three people down there."

"Firefighters?"

"Don't seem to be. I'm going in for a closer look."

"Jeff, the fire's spreading this way, fast."

"It'll just take a minute."

Jeff dipped the plane. He saw a car parked on the shoulder, and three figures lying in a roadside picnic area. They were not moving. "Tim, I'm going to land the plane on the road and take a closer look."

"Jeff, the fire's too close! You'll get burned!"

"It's not that close, yet. I think I have time."

"Jeff, even if the fire doesn't get you, it may be too hot for you to take off."

"I don't have to take off," Jeff said. "All I have to do is taxi down the road."

"The fire's spreading too fast!"

Jeff, however, had already circled the plane into a landing position.

"Jeff, they may already be dead!"

"And they may not."

"You're crazy, Jeff, you know that."

"May be." The plane landed smoothly on the highway and Jeff braked to a stop near the picnic area. As quickly as he could, he got out and ran to the figures. A radio blared out music. Food scraps lay on the ground everywhere. A beer keg had been placed in the cleft of a large rock. Jeff went to the first man, who was not any older than Jeff, if that old. He shook him. The man groaned but did not open his eyes. "Come on, get up, there's a fire!" He did the same to the second man, and the third, but nothing could rouse them. They reeked with the smell of beer and hard liquor—Jeff also saw bottles of whiskey nearby.

Jeff still wore his earpiece. "Jeff, you gotta get out of there!" Tim urged.

At five foot eleven, Jeff could bench press 200 pounds, and all that muscle was put to the test as he lifted each man using a fireman's carry and dumped them into the plane. Hurriedly, he strapped himself into the pilot's seat and started the engines.

"Jeff, the fire's coming up right behind you!"

He taxied eastward, keeping an eye on the monitor on the instrument panel. The camera on the tail showed that Tim had not been exaggerating—the flames were rapidly catching up.

Jeff accelerated to maximum, making fast forward progress, but otherwise all the plane did was hop up and down on the highway, the fire reaching for the plane all the way.

Suddenly, a gust of wind from the east lifted the wings. "Come on, baby, come on!" Jeff said, and climbed up from the highway...higher...higher....another surge of wind...and he was up again!

"Whew!" Tim let out a breath.

"Okay, let's go!" Jeff had not cleared the firebreak, however, when the port engine sputtered.

"Oh, no!" Tim said, noticing.

"I can get home on one engine," Jeff said.

"Provided the other one doesn't go out."

"Then I'll glide in." He looked down. "But I think I'll unload my passengers, just in case. There's an aid station near here. We can call them to pick up these guys."

Again, Jeff landed on the highway...the area had been evacuated for miles around. With the huge firebreak now between them and the blaze, Jeff felt safe taking out the men and settling them in a grassy area next to the road. He took a toolkit and looked at the sputtering engine.

"See anything?" Tim said from his vantage point, circling above Jeff and his plane.

"There's dust and ash clogging the mechanism, not surprising. I'll clear it out the best I can but it'll probably go out again before we reach base."

"As long as you can take off, you can make it."

And he did. Once in the air, Jeff radioed the aid station to pick up the men.

"Any idea who they were?" Tim said as they flew back to base.

"Guys from the university, I think, judging from their jackets and t-shirts."

"University emblem, eh?"

"Yeah."

"They picked a dangerous place to party."

"Well, the fire was a long way away last night, and there would be no one to arrest them, since the area was evacuated."

"Still, pretty stupid, if you ask me."

"No more stupid than that stink bomb you planted in the locker room of the visiting team during the big game."

Tim chuckled. "You had to remind me of that!"

Jeff's engine sputtered again. "There it goes."

"We're almost back at base."

Jeff radioed for permission to land and explained his difficulty. The tower let him land before Tim; touchdown was a bit awkward, but Jeff put the plane in the hangar without further incident. He talked to the mechanics, and walked over to Tim as Tim left his plane.

The commandant came in. After both cadets saluted, and got an "at ease," she said, "Good work, both of you. I'll be sure that both of you get a commendation, and that the Governor hears of it."

"Thank you, ma'am," they answered.

"Take the rest of the weekend off. You've earned it."

"Yes, ma'am!"

"Dismissed."

They walked back to senior quarters. As they walked into the lounge, which was empty, they saw that the television had been left on. Jeff stopped.

"What is it?" Tim asked.

"Those are the guys I rescued at the side of the road."

"Oh, really?" Tim turned to the television.

One of the students said to the television reporter, "If it wasn't for the aid workers finding us, we would have been fried!"

"How do you like that!" Tim said. "They're taking credit for your rescue!"

Jeff waved a hand. "Doesn't matter." He turned to go to their room.

Tim followed. "You ought to call the television station and tell them what really happened."

"Then they'd just think I was grandstanding," Jeff said. "We're getting a commendation, that's all the recognition I need."

"Sometimes I wonder about you, Jeff." He put a hand on Jeff's shoulder. "Maybe I could call the station."

Jeff shook his head. "It's just our word. Without their remembering me, there's really no proof."

"I guess so...but I still think it's unfair."

When they reached their room, Tim took off his hat and flight jacket and slumped into a chair. "What do you want to do now?"

"This is the last night of the concert series over at the university. I thought I'd go see it."

Tim scratched his head. "Well, you know I'm not the classical music type." He sat up straight. "Hey, I just remembered...this is the opening weekend of that new action movie." He checked his watch. "Just have time to catch the next showing." He grabbed his jacket again and hurried out.

Since he did not own a suit, Jeff changed into his uniform and drove his 10-year-old car to the university. He bought a ticket for himself, and found his seat near the front, between two couples. The curtain was closed, but he could hear the musicians tuning their instruments from behind it. He applauded with the others when it opened. The musicians bowed, and the conductor introduced a piece by Mozart. As the music played, Jeff's eyes wandered to the orchestra members, and fixed on the pianist. She was beautiful—a brown-haired, slim woman who appeared to be around his age. Soon, he could hear nothing but the piano, see nothing but the pianist as she swayed in time with the music. She smiled through the entire concert as if she was savoring every note. Jeff found himself floating away on a musical stream....

"Sir?" an usher interrupted his reverie.

"Huh? Hm?" he faced the young man, who was leaning toward him from the aisle.

"The concert is over. We're closing."

Jeff glanced around the room, suddenly realizing he was the only audience member left in the hall. "Oh. Sorry." He picked up his hat and stood. As he angled his way toward the aisle, he saw the pianist gathering her music. He walked toward the stage. "Ma'am, that's the best performance I ever heard."

She smiled at him. "Thank you. It's always nice to have an appreciative audience."

He took the smile as an invitation and strode up the stairs to the stage. "Can I buy you a cup of coffee? There's a coffee shop just across the street."

Still smiling, she looked him up and down. "I've heard about you Air Force cadets...that a girl isn't safe around you."

Unfortunately, he knew exactly what she meant. Two of his senior-year classmates had already been expelled from the Academy for bad behavior, and there were three other cadets who were paying child support for kids they hardly knew, by mothers they had long since broken up with. He straightened up at attention and said with all the sincerity he could muster, "You'll always be safe with me."

She paused a moment before answering. Her smile faded slightly, then came back. "All right...Cadet Tracy."

He realized she had read his name badge. He held out a hand. "Jeff Tracy."

She took it. "Lucy Taylor."

He extended an arm. "Shall we?"

"Let me get my sweater." She took her music and left.

He watched her leave, realized that he had let her go. Would she come back? Was that just an excuse? Should he have gone with her? No, that would make it seem as if he were a stalker. If she did not come back, it probably meant she was not interested...or had a boyfriend already. An eternity of seconds later, she reappeared, hurrying toward him, wearing the sweater and carrying her purse. He grinned and extended his arm again. She took it and smiled back.

In the coffee shop, she ordered a latte. He ordered a carafe of black coffee. They found an out-of-the-way table for two and sat.

"So, what do you do now that the series is ended?" Jeff asked.

"Back to class. I just perform evenings and weekends."

"Do you go to the University?"

"Yes. I'm a music major, and a minor in art."

"Senior year?"

"Yes. You?"

Jeff nodded. "Is your family here?"

For the first time, she frowned. "My parents died three years ago, in a car accident. I'm an only child."

"Oh. I'm sorry."

She nodded. "Neither of my parents had siblings, either, and my grandparents are gone. I got a small inheritance, but I'm mostly living on student loans and jobs."

"Do you get paid for the concerts?"

"Yes. Not a lot."

"You seem to enjoy playing the piano."

Her face brightened. "Oh, yes. Music has gotten me through the tough times. Life is never easy, but it can be what we make it." She took a sip of latte. "What about your family?"

"Mom and Dad own a farm in Kansas. I'm an only child, too."

"So, are you going to fly planes when you graduate?"

"Yes, I love flying. I'm going to get into experimental jets, and once I've got that experience under my belt, I'm going to apply to the astronaut corps."

She inhaled sharply. "How exciting! I've always wondered what it would be like to go into space."

"Well, passenger space flights shouldn't be too far away. I'm hoping to get on the ground floor for the planned lunar colony. Some day you could live on the moon, if you wanted to."

"Would you want to?"

"Only if you were there." The words came out of his mouth without his really thinking about it. He wondered if he had been too forward. But she grinned, and he relaxed.

Eventually—it seemed such a short time, and yet, such a long time—he drove her home. For her, home was the senior dorm at the university. She escorted him past security and into the women's wing. As Lucy led the way, other women passed them, turning their heads to look. One gave Lucy a "thumbs up" sign; another said, "Wow, Lucy, where have you been hiding him all this time?" Lucy did not answer her, but said to Jeff, "Just ignore them. They've never seen me bring a man to my room before."

Jeff felt special. Was he the first? At the same time, he could not imagine that other men would not flock around his gorgeous woman. "You don't go on dates?" he asked diplomatically.

Lucy put her key in the door. "Oh, dinner or a movie, occasionally. Nothing serious. I'm busy enough just trying to survive—besides going to classes, playing the piano, and painting."

Jeff was just about to reply that his studies meant he did not date much, either, when he caught her last phrase. "Painting?"

She opened the door and motioned to the walls. His first reaction was that her room was not much larger than the one he shared at the academy with Tim. Then he saw the art. The wall was full of artwork—original artwork. Some were landscapes; some were moonscapes, or Marscapes; and some were shuttles suspended in space. An easel stood against another wall, holding a covered canvas. His jaw dropped. "Did you paint all of these?"

She smiled. "Yes. Do you like them?"

"They're amazing!"

She motioned to a chair. "I'm afraid I just have one chair for guests."

"Oh. That's not necessary. I mean, I'd like to stay longer, but I have to get back to the academy. My car will be ticketed if I stay much longer, and I can't really afford that."

"Oh, yes, I should have known."

"I'd like to see you again, though."

"Me, too." She went to the desk and grabbed a pen and a memo pad. She scribbled and tore off a page. "Here's my number and text messaging address."

He reached around her and took the pen and memo pad. When he was done, he handed her a page. "Here's mine." They exchanged papers. She put his on the desk; he folded hers and put it in his pocket. To Jeff's everlasting surprise and delight, she kissed him. He gently took her in his arms and kissed her back.

"Mmmm, nice," she said when she took a breath.

He pulled back a little. "We'll have to do this again, soon."

She nodded and motioned to the door. "I have to escort you out."

He held out an arm. "I'll escort you."

When they got to the lobby, past security, they saw two students, a man and a woman, across the room. The man held a book above the woman while she snatched at it.

"Ed, give me my book!" the woman insisted.

"Not 'til you say you'll go to the game with me."

"Ed, I said I have to study for my exam!"

"What's more important, Heather, the exam, or me?"

By this time, Jeff had rushed across the room. He grabbed the book from Ed's hand, gave it back to Heather, and positioned himself right in front of Ed. "What's the matter with you? Give the lady the book!"

"You Air Force guys think you can boss anyone around."

"And bullies like you think you can get away with anything." He motioned to the security officer, standing at the door, watching them. "Shall we ask security which one of us she thinks is right?"

"Awwww." He waved his hand and skulked away.

"Thank you," Heather said.

"You're welcome."

Heather left; Lucy walked up to Jeff. "You have a temper on you, Jeff, as my mother used to say."

"Sorry."

"Don't be sorry! The world would be a better place if we all stood up to bullies like that."

With every word she said, he loved her more and more.

A hot bubble of air had passed through Kansas that April, so Jeff decided to fire up the grill in the back yard and cook hot dogs for dinner. The same weather front had collided with a mass of cold air from Canada, causing a blizzard in Alpine City, the posh resort in the Rockies where Lucy was exhibiting her artwork, or else she would have been home by now. In her last call, Lucy had said that the snow had stopped, and the roads had been plowed. She would be taking the hotel's van to the airport, and expected to be home later that evening. The boys were thrilled—especially Scott, whose 13th birthday had been just days before. Lucy had given Scott a box that held only a note, promising that she would buy him the flight simulator for his computer right after she got back. Lucy had confirmed to Jeff over the phone that she had sold more than enough artwork to make the purchase.

As much as Jeff wanted Lucy home, he also relished having some time alone with his sons. He had only been able to return to his modest home three or four times a year between moon missions, and although he e-mailed home and spoke with his sons over webcam—which was awkward with the time delay in communications between Earth and Moon—when he was away, the reunions always seemed awkward. It seemed as if there was always something in his sons' lives that he missed when he was gone, and just as he thought he had caught up, he was off again. While Jeff loved his work building the moon base, he loved his wife and sons even more, and often thought there just had to be a way to combine his two loves more effectively.

Supper preparations continued as the boys smoothed the paper tablecloth over the picnic table and distributed the plates. Jeff had just put the last hot dog in the last open bun and handed the plate to Scott when his cell phone rang. He saw on the readout that it was Lucy.

Without waiting for her to speak first, he said, "That was fast! Are you at the airport already?"

"Jeff...something's happened." Her voice sounded strained.

He felt his skin turn clammy. "Tell me all about it." His mind readied to give whatever solution the problem required.

"The van...went off the road. I think a ridge...above the highway... collapsed under the weight of the snow and hit us."

"Are you all right?"

"No." Her voice was calm.

"What's wrong?"

"Hurt. Can't move, except my right arm. Can't feel my legs."

"Bleeding?"

"Internally, maybe. Something feels funny inside. No blood on my clothes."

"Is anyone helping you?"

"There's no one. The others...don't answer when I call...."

"Okay. Just don't move for now." Jeff turned to John. "John, get upstairs on your radio and call Colorado Emergency Services. Give them your Mom's cell phone number and tell them to track her GPS."

John nodded and stood.

"I need to talk to John!" Lucy said desperately.

Jeff motioned John over. He held the phone to John's ear, but angled so he could still hear Lucy himself.

"I'm here, Mom."

"John...I want you to promise me...when you grow up...you choose what you want to do...not what you think someone else wants you to."

"I will, Mom."

"I love you, John."

"I love you, too, Mom."

Jeff took the phone back and whispered, "Go...go."

John nodded and ran.

"Now listen to me, Angel," Jeff said. "You're going to be fine. Someone will come very soon."

"I want to talk to the boys."

Scott, Virgil, and Gordon had lined up beside Jeff. Three-year-old Alan continued to eat his hot dog at the table. Jeff gave the phone to Scott. "Keep your mother talking," Jeff said in a low voice.

Scott nodded. "Mom...."

"Scott. You tell Dad you're entitled to that flight simulator."

"I don't care about the flight simulator, Mom. Just come home."

"I love you, Scott."

"I love you, too, Mom."

Jeff gestured at his second son. "Virgil," he whispered.

"Hi, Mom!"

"Virgil...don't be shy about telling Scott and your father that you want to be an astronaut, too."

Scott turned to Virgil and said excitedly, "Virgil!"

Virgil looked a bit embarrassed, but said, "Okay, Mom."

"I love you, Virgil."

"I love you, too, Mom." Virgil gave the phone to Gordon.

"Hi, Mom," Gordon said.

Lucy answered slowly, but distinctly. "Gordon, remember... you don't have to go to college if you don't want to. If you want to enlist in the Navy or join the aquanauts right out of high school...tell your father that I said that was all right."

"Okay, Mom."

"I love you, Gordon."

"I love you, too, Mom."

Jeff brought the phone over to Alan, who had continued eating all this time. He put the phone up to Alan's face. "Alan, your mom wants to talk to you."

Alan turned until his lips nearly touched the phone. "Come home, Mommy!"

"I love you, Alan."

"I love you too, Mommy!" Alan shouted into the receiver. "Come home!" He went back to eating.

Jeff took the phone back. "Angel, I need to know where you are. Are you still in the van, or outside?"

"Outside. In the snow."

"Is your coat on?"

"Yes. I'm sort of under the van. I think a bunch of rocks hit it. It's in pieces."

"The important thing is to stay awake."

"Yes. Ohhhh..."

"What?" Jeff said. When Lucy did not answer, he said, "Angel, talk to me. Angel. Say something."

"I love you, Jeff." He could barely hear her. "Take care of the boys."

"I love you, too, Angel. We'll take care of the boys together."

"Ohhh...." Another groan.

The phone went dead.

Jeff desperately tried to call back, but could not get anything. Scott, Virgil, and Gordon looked on anxiously.

John ran toward them. "Dad...," he took a breath. "They're on their way."

Jeff reached out and put a hand on his arm. "All right. Good work. Sit down and finish your supper." He looked at his other sons. "Boys, you need to eat. You won't help your mother by starving yourselves."

Scott sat, but said, "They'll get to Mom okay, won't they Dad?"

"Sure. Sure they will." Jeff turned to his food, but his thoughts were elsewhere.

"Dad?"

"Hm?" He looked up at Scott, and realized that he had lost track of time. His dinner was still untouched, cold. He found he was not hungry, anyway. Looking up, he saw John and Virgil quietly clearing the table.

"What's for dessert?" Alan asked. "I want ice cream."

There was nothing to do but wait for a call. They played a video of Alan's favorite movie, which featured talking cars. No one but Alan paid attention. The rest of them sat on the sofa, just staring out into space, saying nothing.

Countdown to Action! 19

Finally, the phone rang. Jeff walked over to get it. "Jeff Tracy speaking."

A gray-haired woman appeared on the telecall screen. "Mr. Tracy? This is Mercy Hospital. I'm terribly sorry. I'm afraid I have bad news for you, Mr. Tracy...."

When the call ended, he saw his four eldest sons standing in the doorway of the kitchen, looking on anxiously. Jeff walked toward them, and put his arms around them, two sons on each side. "Come on, let's sit down."

Alan did not understand. "But why can't Mommy come home?" he would say, even after they explained. When Jeff called his mother over to watch the boys while he flew to Colorado to get Lucy, Alan screamed that he wanted Mommy, not Grandma. Once Lucy's body had been transferred to the funeral parlor, Jeff sat at the kitchen table with the boys, going over the arrangements. Alan became hysterical over the idea that Mommy would be buried, even if she would be buried next to Grandpa. They found a space in a mausoleum, instead. When they went to the visitation, surrounded by Jeff's fellow astronauts and their spouses, Alan pushed a chair over to the coffin, climbed up, and pounded on Lucy's chest. "Mommy, wake up!" he shouted. Jeff had to carry him out, kicking and screaming. The coffin was closed for the service. Alan had calmed down by then, and watched silently when the coffin was interred. Jeff thought that was the end of it. But a couple of weeks later, Alan walked up to Jeff after breakfast. "Daddy, can we go and bring Mommy home, now?"

Jeff did not answer. He sat at the table, head in his hands. Every time the wound seemed to be closing, Alan would open it again. The other boys had tried to explain death to their younger brother, too, but Alan did not believe them. Jeff had done his best to remain calm around the boys, confining his crying jags to when he was alone in the shower. As for the other boys, though they had cried and questioned and ranted about the unfairness of it all, at least he was able to get through to them. Then he remembered that NASA had a counseling service that he could call 24 hours a day. They had to have some answers for them.

As he reached for the phone, it rang. He had not been expecting a call; the condolence calls had long since stopped. "Jeff Tracy."

A woman about Lucy's age appeared on the screen. "Mr. Tracy, this is Alice Edgerton, Lucy's agent. I don't know if you remember me; I saw you at the funeral, but there were a lot of people there."

"Oh, yes," he said, though he had not remembered.

"Mr. Tracy, now that some time has passed, I wanted to warn you that you might be getting calls about Lucy's paintings."

"Why?"

"The value of an artist's work always goes up when an artist dies, and I wanted to be sure that you didn't part with them for less than they're worth. I can help you with this, if you want."

"Do you think I care about that!" he growled, and terminated the call. He turned and saw Alan, still there, looking at him expectantly. "Alan," he said, as softly as he could, "we'll talk about Mommy later."

"Won't Mommy ever come home?" he said sadly.

Jeff sighed heavily. "We'll talk later, son. You run along." After Alan slinked away, he dialed the counseling service. "This is Jeff Tracy. I need your help."

A woman wearing glasses appeared on the screen. "Yes, Mr. Tracy. I heard about your wife, it was in all the papers. I'm so sorry. How can I help?"

"It's my son. My youngest son, Alan. He thinks his Mother is still alive. He keeps asking for her, and I don't know what to do. Can you tell me how to explain it to him?"

"And how are you doing, Mr. Tracy?"

"I'm not talking about me, I'm talking about my son!"

"Let me schedule an appointment for you, Mr. Tracy. You sound pretty shaken, yourself."

Jeff terminated the connection. No one understood. He dialed Tim Casey.

"Jeff, you're a mess," Tim said after Jeff explained.

Jeff rubbed his forehead. "I don't know what to do."

"You need to take some time off, by yourself."

"I can't leave the boys, not now!"

"You're no use to them as you are, either. You've had a shock, and you need some R&R to recover. Now, I and some of the others here at the base have a timeshare in Singapore. It's empty right now and I'll give you my key codes. Inside you'll find a map. There's a real quiet, restful place in Malaysia where we go and just decompress. It's a day trip; just rent a car and pack a lunch. You'll be all the better for it."

Jeff sighed. "All right. I'll call my mother to watch the boys."

Scott walked in on him as he was packing. "Where are you going, Dad? I didn't know there was another launch scheduled."

"No, son, I'm still on bereavement leave. I'm going to Singapore."

"But Dad, what if something happens to you?"

He turned to Scott. "Nothing's going to happen to me, son. I know that you're anxious because of your mother, but we can't spend the rest of our lives in a cocoon. Many people spend all of their lives driving or flying and never have an accident bad enough to even send them to the hospital."

Scott looked stricken. "Are you leaving because of me?"

"No, son!" Jeff said, genuinely surprised.

Scott walked over and hugged his father. "I'm sorry, Dad. It was my fault. If I hadn't asked for that flight simulator, Mom would never have gone to Colorado."

Jeff patted Scott on the back. "No, son, that's not it at all. Your mother would have gone anyway, she'd planned on that exhibition for months." Jeff held Scott at arm's length so he could look him in the eye. "Son, it was my fault your mother died. I could have flown her to and from the exhibition myself. There was a small airfield just down the road from the hotel."

"But Dad, I thought your plane was being repaired."

Jeff's private jet, purchased with the inheritance he had received when his father died and his mother sold the farm, was the only real asset the family had, besides the house and the two cars. Like Scott, Jeff had been waiting for Lucy to bring home some revenue so he could afford to get it fixed. In fact, he found later that the money had been transferred to their joint account before Lucy had even left the hotel; the plane was now airworthy again.

"One of the other astronauts would have loaned me a plane, if I'd asked, I'm sure."

Scott shook his head. "It wasn't your fault, either, Dad."

"Son, if I'd just been there, your mother would have been safe."

"But I heard Grandma tell you there was nothing you could have done to prevent Mom dying...it was just an accident, nothing more."

Jeff just looked at the ceiling and shook his head.

"Please don't go, Dad."

He looked back at Scott. "I need to, son. I need to be alone. It's not that I don't love you and your brothers...I do. It's hard to explain, and I know it's hard for you to understand. Just know that it's for a short time and I'll be back. Your Grandma will take care of you while I'm gone."

"Well, okay, Dad," Scott said, but he still looked confused.

Once Jeff was in the air, he felt himself again. Flying always had this soothing effect on him, and space flight even more so. He looked forward to going to Singapore—he had been there with Tim when they were flying experimental aircraft for the Air Force. It was a place where he knew no one, and no one would know him except perhaps as a face they had seen in the news. Maybe Tim was right—he could think there, and figure out what he would do for the rest of his life.

He landed safely in Singapore, and took a day to get adjusted to the time difference. During that time, he stuck to the shops and restaurants with which he was familiar. A major technology center, Singapore electronics shops offered many intriguing gadgets, some of which he purchased for his sons: a battery-powered kiddie car for Alan, a radio controlled boat for Gordon, a high-powered sender/receiver for John, a model rocket for Virgil, and a programmable two-foot-high robot for Scott.

The next day, he rented a jeep and took the map/GPS to guide him on the way. As Tim suggested, he went to a restaurant and ordered a take out lunch and a thermos of coffee before getting on the road. The Malaysian border guard checked his identity card and waved him through. Within the hour, the highway became a road, which, after some twists and turns, became a gravel path. Jeff reduced speed to a crawl as the vegetation on both sides of the road became more dense.

At last, the GPS told him he had arrived at his destination. He put the jeep in park, pocketed his sunglasses, took his lunch, and stepped out in to a wide clearing with stone ruins. Consulting the guidebook that Tim left for him, he read that this had been an ancient retreat for royalty, abandoned for centuries. Walking around, he saw wide steps leading to a platform, presumably the foundation for the main building. He also saw a huge field of gorgeous flowers, grown tall, almost waist height. Jeff had no idea what the name of the flowers might be, but they ranged in color from purple to red to orange to yellow. Their subtle scent filled the air.

Jeff sat on the top—fourth—step to eat his lunch and drink his coffee. A warm, moist breeze blew around him, caressing his skin. As he became attuned to the sights and sounds, he noticed a river running just beyond the field of flowers. The sound of the rush of water soothed his nerves. He moved his shoulders up and down, back and forth, as the tension in his muscles eased. He blew out a long breath. Yes, it was very peaceful here.

The soft noise of a small motor caught his attention. Glancing at his watch, he was surprised to see that he had been sitting there for about two hours. He stood to ease his muscles and saw a man in a small boat coming to the shore. The man stopped the motor, stepped out, and tied the boat to the tree. Then he walked into the field of flowers, carrying what appeared to be a small machete. He had not seemed to have noticed Jeff at all.

Jeff expected the man to gather flowers, but instead, as he watched, the man seemed to be cutting weeds. Once in a while, he would stop, examine a petal, and trim the plant without harming a bloom. Or he would bend down out of Jeff's sight, and come up again, tossing some dead brush, or perhaps a rock, aside. He was gardening!

Intrigued by the man's work, he strode down the steps. First, he packed his trash in the paper bag he carried his lunch in and stowed it in the jeep with the thermos. Then he picked his way through the flower field. It was slow going, since the plants were high and close together. Suddenly, he slipped on some loose dirt and found himself falling.

Splash! He fell into water, feet first, and found himself submerged. His first thought was that this must be an abandoned well. When he tried to swim to the surface, however, he found himself being sucked down. A drain? As much as he struggled, he could not make any headway. He was running out of air. All he could think was that if he did not reach the surface soon, his sons would be orphans....

2

Dizzy from lack of air, Jeff stopped swimming. A rapid current carried him backwards. Just as he was on the verge of losing consciousness, he felt a hand grab the collar at the back of his leather jacket, pulling him up. He broke the surface and gasped for air.

The hand released him.

Panting, Jeff found himself lying on his stomach on a sandy flat next to the river. He looked up to see a Malaysian man—the one he saw gardening earlier—peering down at him.

"Are you all right?" asked the man. He spoke in clear English, only slightly accented.

Jeff nodded. "Yes. Just a bit shaken." Slowly, he pulled himself into a sitting position. Looking up the embankment, he saw the stairs where he had eaten his lunch. "How did I get here?"

"An ancient storm drain." The man pointed. "It carries rainwater from up at the ruins to the river. When there is no rain, there is still water from an underground stream."

Jeff looked toward the river and saw a torrent rushing from a brick-lined hole from the side of the hill into the river. That was what the man must have pulled him out of. Then he looked back to the hill. "The opening up there ought to be covered...or at least, someone should put up a sign."

"There is a cover, and a sign."

"I never saw it."

"Treasure hunters sometimes come here seeking valuables, though these ruins were looted centuries ago. They must have removed them when digging around it, since I was last here. I will go and replace them. You rest here."

Jeff did not argue, he still felt a bit weak and breathless. He watched as the man strode up the hill. He could not see everything the man did because of the height of the plants, but eventually he saw what appeared to be the top of a sign.

The man returned. Jeff noticed that his rescuer was a thin man, shorter than himself. He wore a traditional robe and footwear. As he approached, Jeff stood. "Thank you for helping me." He held out a hand. "Jeff Tracy."

The man took and shook it. "Kyrano."

"Is that your first or last name?"

Kyrano smiled. "It is my only name, Jeff Tracy." He motioned to the boat. "Why not come home with me? It is not far; you can call the rental company to pick up the vehicle."

Jeff considered. Why not, indeed? "Okay, thanks."

Kyrano gestured to a seat inside the boat. Jeff climbed in while Kyrano untied the boat and got in himself. As he sat in the driver's seat and started the motor, Jeff looked around. He saw that covered baskets, packages, bags, and parcels had been stacked in the bow near the boat's steering wheel and control panel.

Once they were on their way, Kyrano reached for a towel and handed it to Jeff. He rubbed his hair with it and folded it, placing it on an empty seat. It was a hot day; his clothes dried quickly. He took off his leather jacket, too.

"How far do we need to go?" Jeff asked.

"Only 2 kilometers more."

"Do you come to the ruins often?"

"When I am out shopping, yes. It is good for my soul to tend the flowers."

"They're beautiful. You do a good job."

"I wished to honor those who first planted them, centuries ago. The local government used to tend the area as a nature preserve, but the government officials changed and decided that it was too expensive to keep up."

"The same thing happens where I come from."

They proceeded up the river quietly after that, both men taking in the stillness.

Soon Jeff saw a wooden dock extending into the river. A little girl about Alan's age ran toward the boat as Kyrano tied it up. "Papa! Papa!" she said.

Kyrano stepped on the dock and scooped up the little girl in his arms. He said something to her in a language Jeff did not understand; he presumed it was the local dialect. When Jeff stepped on the dock, he saw a slim woman walking toward them. She wore a v-necked white blouse and knee-length khakis. She kissed Kyrano on the cheek.

"Collette," Kyrano said to the woman, "this is Jeff Tracy. He fell into the drain at the ruins."

Jeff bowed and extended a hand. "Pleased to meet you, ma'am."

She took it. "Are you all right?" she asked. She had a distinct French accent.

"Just a little wet. Kyrano, here, saved my life."

"Oh, I just gave you a little help," Kyrano said modestly.

Jeff turned to Collette. "He really did save me. I was just about out of air."

Kyrano turned to Jeff. "This is my wife, Collette, and my daughter, Tin-Tin."

"Very pleased to meet you both. They're both lovely," Jeff added to Kyrano, and meant it.

"You are most kind, Jeff Tracy." Collette looked at him. "Are you the astronaut, by any chance?"

"Yes, ma'am."

"Oh, but you must call me Collette."

"Then you must call me Jeff."

"I told Jeff Tracy he could rest here and call the rental company to pick up his vehicle," Kyrano said.

Jeff reached into his shirt. Whenever he was away from home, he carried his wallet, passport, and cell phone in a weatherproof pouch next to his skin. "I have my phone with me."

Collette touched Jeff's arm. "But first, you must shower and change."

"Uh...," Both Kyrano and Collette were smaller than he; although Kyrano wore a light, loose robe, Jeff could not see himself fitting into their clothes.

Collette waved at him. "Come."

Jeff followed closely as Kyrano led the way, still carrying Tin-Tin, who had rested her head on his shoulder. Collette took Kyrano's free arm. Jeff felt a pang of grief for Lucy as he saw the two sweethearts strolling along the path.

Because of the closely-spaced trees, Jeff did not see the house until they were almost at the doorstep. It was a large, two-story white house of local architecture. Beyond it, Jeff could see smaller, comfortable cottages, also of local architecture, and more people walking around. Kyrano spoke to some of them, again in local dialect, directing them toward the boat. Jeff had the impression that Kyrano must be a farmer and the other people must be the farm hands, whom he had directed to unload the boat.

Once inside, Kyrano handed Tin-Tin to Collette with a reassuring word, and escorted Jeff to a room upstairs, inviting Jeff to take a shower and rest. Then he left, closing the door behind him. When Jeff emerged from the shower, he found clean clothes laid out on the bed. The pants had an adjustable waistline; the shirt an adjustable front. Jeff guessed that the Kyranos often entertained visitors.

Once dressed, he sat in a chair near a window and called home. Scott answered the phone, told Jeff everyone was fine there, but wanted him to come home soon. Jeff decided not to tell him about the incident with the drain. Instead, he told Scott he was now staying with someone in Malaysia, told him to tell his Grandma and his brothers, and said he would call again soon.

Jeff's phone could access a worldwide directory, and soon he was talking to the rental agency, which had an English-speaking staff. They said they would find the jeep using the GPS and pick it up for a nominal extra charge. Jeff agreed to let them add it to his bill.

Feeling exhausted, he lay on the bed, thinking only to take a quick nap before rejoining his hosts.

When he opened his eyes, he saw Kyrano placing a tray on a table at the other end of the room. Raising his head, he realized that someone had tucked a pillow under it. He also saw someone had placed a blanket over him.

Kyrano turned to him and smiled. "Good morning, Jeff Tracy."

Jeff sat up, rubbing his chin, which had stubble on it. "You mean I slept all evening?"

"Yes, and through the night, too," Kyrano said warmly. "You needed the rest. It's just after 5 a.m." He indicated the tray. "Would you like some coffee?"

"Sure." Jeff stumbled over, amazed at how weak his legs seemed to be, and sat at the table.

Kyrano poured out a cup from a coffee pot. "Cream or sugar?"

"No, thanks." Jeff took a sip, then drew back his head in surprise. "This is the best coffee I've ever tasted! What is it?"

"Oh, I grind it fresh. We grow a little coffee here."

"It's heavenly!" He buttered a croissant and bit into it. "Oh, oh, oh," he said between bites. "This is...," he swallowed. "This is great! My compliments to the chef."

"Thank you."

"You're the chef?"

A voice spoke from the door. "Kyrano is a world-class chef. That's how we met," Collette said proudly.

Kyrano walked over to her and took her hand. "Collette was a ballerina. She came to the restaurant where I worked in Paris."

"I had to meet the chef who had cooked such a delicious meal."

"What brought you here...if it's not too personal a question?"

"Not at all," Kyrano said. "My father was dying. He asked if I would take over the farm. My degree is in botany. After chef's school, I wanted to work with the freshest food."

Jeff nodded. "Sorry to hear about your father."

"He married late, then married again after my mother died. He lived a full and happy life."

"Is his second wife still around?"

Kyrano's sunny expression faded, and Collette frowned. "There was an automobile accident," she said simply.

"Oh, sorry."

"We will let you eat," Kyrano said. "You must be hungry."

"I am. And thank you."

After eating, Jeff made another call home. This time his mother answered. "Jeff! We were so worried."

"Worried? Didn't Scott tell you I was okay?"

"Yes, but when we called back, you didn't answer."

"Oh." He scratched an eyebrow. "I fell asleep, and just woke up. I must have been more tired than I thought."

"When will you be home? The boys miss you."

"As soon as I can. I just need to get back to Singapore. I'll call again when I'm ready to come back."

"Alan wants to talk to you."

"Okay."

"Daddy?"

"Hi, Alan. Are you being a good boy for Grandma?"

"Please come home, Daddy. Please. I promise I'll be good. I promise I won't ask for Mommy again."

Jeff sighed. He lowered the phone and rubbed his forehead.

"Please, Daddy."

Jeff took a breath to compose himself. "Daddy will be home as soon as he can. We'll all be together. I promise." He heard his mother say, "Now, run along, Alan," before she got back on the phone. "No one told him to say that, Jeff. He just asked to talk to Daddy. I thought he would just say hello."

"I know."

"Call back when you can, Jeff."

"I will. I'm sorry it's so hard on the boys."

"They miss you, Jeff. I do too."

"Give them my love."

"I will."

"I have to say bye for now, Mother. I'll call later."

By the time Jeff shaved and washed, he felt better. He walked downstairs and found Kyrano and Collette standing at a counter in a spacious, glistening kitchen. The pair looked somber, in contrast to their daughter, who happily drew pictures at the kitchen table.

Thinking he might have become an inconvenience, Jeff walked over. "I can be off as soon as I can find someone to take me to the Singapore."

They both looked surprised. "You needn't leave us so soon," Collette said.

"You're welcome to stay as long as you wish," Kyrano added.

"No, I should get home soon. My family needs me. I lost my wife just a short time ago, and we're all still adjusting."

Collette put a hand on Jeff's upper arm. "I am so sorry."

Jeff nodded.

Kyrano stepped behind Jeff and put his hands on Jeff's shoulders. "Here. You should sit and rest awhile."

"Uh...," Jeff started to protest, but it got him nowhere. Despite the fact that he was taller and heavier than Kyrano, he found that he could not resist Kyrano's gentle push as the other man guided him into a sitting room and into a chair. "I'll bring coffee," he said. Shortly thereafter, he came back with a tray and coffee pot. He and Collette sat on a couch opposite Jeff with the coffee on a table between them. "Your grief must be very great to bring you so far from your home."

Jeff felt touched by their sympathy. He found himself telling them his story, how wonderful life had been with Lucy, how proud they were of their five sons, how devastated they had all been by her death. When he was done, Kyrano came over and put his hand on Jeff's arm. "You will heal from this, Jeff Tracy."

For the first time, Jeff felt that he could. Before he was able to reply, however, he heard a loud car horn beeping repeatedly, accompanied by the sound of panicked animals. "What's that?" he said, looking out the window. Dust showed a car careening down a dirt road toward them. Poultry and cattle scattered out of its path. Turning back toward the kitchen, he saw Kyrano hurry to the table there and speak softly to Tin-Tin. Her face brightened and she ran out the back door.

"It's Kyrano's half-brother," Collette explained to Jeff as they watched Tin-Tin leave. "She does not know she has an uncle. We send her out to play whenever he comes."

"Is he abusive?" Jeff asked.

"He is a bad influence altogether," she replied. "He is known as 'The Hood' around here."

"'Hood' is American slang for 'criminal,'" Jeff said.

"And that is what he is." She nodded out the window as the honking grew louder. "He is the world's worst driver...just as his mother was. It's a miracle he hasn't crashed himself."

"Does he drive drunk?"

"No," Collette explained, "But she did. She was an Englishwoman who only married Kyrano's father for his money."

"Collette," Kyrano said mildly, "Jeff Tracy does not need to be burdened with our troubles."

"I'm sorry," Collette said to Jeff. "He just makes me so mad! He tries to take advantage of my husband's good nature."

"There is nothing he can do to change my nature," Kyrano assured her.

Jeff motioned toward the door where Tin-Tin had just ran out. "I can go take a walk...."

"There is no need, Jeff Tracy. He will not be staying long." Kyrano walked to the front door and stepped out on the porch. Collette followed; Jeff tagged along. Amid much honking and squealing of brakes, a state-of-the-art land rover came to a stop. A bald man with thick black eyebrows stepped out. He wore a traditional robe. Walking to the bottom of the steps, he spread out his arms as his face broke into a wide smile.

"Kyrano! Brother! How good to see you! And Collette! How lovely you look today!"

Jeff noted that he spoke English, with only a slight accent.

"How's the arms business?" Collette asked dryly.

The Hood chuckled as he put his arms down and walked up the stairs to meet them. "Always joking." He spied Jeff and paused as he reached the landing. "I see you have a visitor."

Jeff extended a hand. "Jeff Tracy."

"The astronaut?" An eager, hungry look crossed his face momentarily. "Bela Ghat." His expression changed to one of concern. "Oh, but you lost your wife recently. I saw it on the television news. I'm so sorry." He shook Jeff's hand with both of his, and released it.

"Thank you," Jeff said cautiously. He did not feel that the condolences were quite sincere.

"What brings you here today, brother?" Kyrano asked.

Ghat handed Kyrano a paper. "The judge has reconsidered our father's will. There will be a hearing tomorrow to decide who inherits."

"Impossible!" Collette exclaimed. "We already proved the will giving Kyrano the lands was the genuine one."

"But I have since found another copy which is dated later."

Kyrano read the paper. "I am sure this is just an error. I will come to the hearing."

Ghat opened his arms expansively. "Why not spare your family another trial? You spent a lot of money with the last one; another could leave you with little to support yourself. Just sign the land over to me and you can still maintain a very comfortable living with what is in your bank account."

Collette sighed explosively. She seemed too angry even to speak.

"I will come to the hearing," Kyrano said calmly. He folded the paper and pocketed it.

Ghat shook his head slightly. "I am only looking out for your interests, brother. The land will be mine, you know this. Why not make it easy for yourself and your loved ones?"

"I will see you tomorrow, brother." Kyrano turned and walked back into the house.

Collette extended her arm. "Leave!"

"Very well." He got back into the vehicle and sped away, honking at anything that came near his intended path.

Jeff did not feel as if he knew enough about the situation to comment on the conversation while it was going on. He turned to Collette and said, "Anything I can do?"

"He does not need the land," Collette said. "He only wants it because he wants to control everything. Anything Kyrano has, he wants that much and more!"

Kyrano stood at the doorway. "He is not worthy of so much attention, my love. When we allow him to make us angry, we allow him to have power over us. I will give him no power over me." He kissed Collette on the cheek.

"You are right, of course," Collette said. "But what do we do? He is right—the cost of another trial will ruin us!"

"All we need do is show up with our documents," Kyrano said. "They have been validated. He only wishes to feel important by putting demands on our time. The judge will then tell him to go away, as he did before."

"But why did the judge reconsider? Kyrano, he must have used those hypnotic drugs on him!"

"Hypnotic drugs?" Jeff asked.

Kyrano, his arm around Collette, turned to Jeff. "My brother has claimed that he has developed the powers of his mind. He says that he can get anyone to do whatever he wishes."

"He has a very slick manner," Jeff said. "Some people are masters of manipulation. Con artists get what they want all the time, just through talking."

"I think it is more than that," Collette said. "He sells illegal arms, and I think that he has access to hypnotic drugs—the kind that armies use for covert operations and interrogating prisoners."

"Well," Jeff said, "I've been informed of such drugs, and they can break down someone's resistance, but they aren't always as reliable as rumored."

Kyrano gave Collette a one-armed hug. "Come, let us not let my brother ruin our day. We will go to the hearing tomorrow. All will be well."

That evening, as Jeff relaxed in his room, he smelled something burning. His first thought was that Kyrano must be in the kitchen, and had spilled something on a hot stove. He walked to the bedroom door and pulled it open; immediately he felt heat coming up from the stairwell. At the same time, he heard Tin-Tin calling, "Papa! Papa!" He rushed downstairs, and slid on the landing, falling to his knees. It was hard for him to get his footing; he sat on the first step and activated the "Sure Tread" feature on his boots, which were supposed to give the soles a firm grip on any surface. Carefully, he made his way to the sitting room, where Kyrano was sprawled on the floor, also trying to get to his feet. Tin-Tin stood beside him, crying. Smoke began to pour in from the kitchen. Jeff helped Kyrano up, then picked up Tin-Tin. With his free arm, he guided Kyrano to the window; he opened it and helped them out. As he jumped the few feet to the ground, he felt heat behind him. A thick black cloud of smelly smoke streamed out the window. "Come on, we have to get away from the house," he said. When they had gone about 10 yards, Jeff turned back. Now he could see flames and sparks. The farm workers had already moved the crop sprinklers and had adjusted the water volume and height so that the structure was being doused from the roof on down.

Meanwhile, Kyrano hurriedly went from one person to the other. "Collette? Collette!" he called. When Jeff saw Kyrano turn toward the house, he ran toward the other man and grabbed him with both arms. "No! You can't go back! You have to think of Tin-Tin!"

"Collette! Oh, Collette!" Kyrano cried in anguish. Then he rested his head on Jeff's shoulder and sobbed. Jeff embraced the smaller man as he would a brother, and found himself in tears, too.

* * *

Someone had apparently called the authorities, but by the time the police and fire vehicles arrived, the fire was out and the house was a charred mess. Tin-Tin, meanwhile, tearfully asked Kyrano the same question over and over; Jeff caught "Mama" and knew what she was asking. Kyrano sat on the ground, took her in his arms, and spoke softly to her. They cried together until she fell asleep. A woman worker eventually came with a mat and blanket; Kyrano put Tin-Tin on the mat, covered her, sat next to her, and just stared silently out into the darkness.

Another worker turned on floodlights; Jeff could see clearly as the investigators sifted through the rubble. With nothing else to do, and the pouch with his only possessions safely inside his shirt, he just sat next to Kyrano and watched.

Eventually, a man in a uniform came up to Kyrano. He began to speak, but Kyrano did not respond. Jeff did not understand what he was saying; when the man turned to him, he shrugged and said, "Sorry, I don't speak the language."

"Are you a friend of the family?" the man asked in English.

Jeff supposed he must be, by now. "Yes."

"I am told the woman we found is this man's wife."

"Yes."

"I am so very sorry. The medical examiner says that it looks as if she slipped and hit her head. She was unconscious and unable to leave; he believes she died of breathing smoke."

Jeff nodded.

"The fire seems to have started in the kitchen. There was incense burning near a statue of the Buddha; that burned down, fell to the floor, and ignited the oil."

"The floor was slippery all over," Jeff said. "It was in the hall and the living room."

The official nodded. "We talked to a housekeeper who had left the house at the request of the woman to get cleaning supplies. She said they had discovered the leak after they had brought in a vat of oil from outside to the kitchen, and that there was a trail of it throughout the house. That is what we found."

The official turned to Kyrano, who had not moved during the entire conversation, and then back to Jeff. "We will take the body to the morgue; your friend can claim it there."

"I'll tell him."

"You may wish to find some help for your friend."

Jeff looked at Kyrano and considered his own grief. He wondered if there was any help for this sort of situation. "Thank you," he said, and the official left.

Eventually, Kyrano stood. Tenderly, he lifted the sleeping Tin-Tin and walked silently toward the worker cottages. Jeff followed. He stopped at a door. "This is our guest cottage, Jeff Tracy. We can stay here."

Jeff opened the door, finding it unlocked. He turned on the lights. The main room was a combination kitchen-dining-sitting room. Beyond that were two small bedrooms and a bath. Kyrano went in one; Jeff went to the other. He found he was exhausted. He slept.

He woke to the smell of coffee. Going to the other room, he found Kyrano making breakfast at the kitchenette. Tin-Tin was already at the table, eating quietly. She looked as if she had been crying again.

Kyrano turned and spoke. "Sit, Jeff Tracy." Jeff did. Kyrano brought and set a plate of eggs and toast in front of him, with a cup of coffee. Then he sat and served himself.

"I was going to leave for Singapore this afternoon," Jeff said. "But I can stay and help here if you need me."

Kyrano shook his head. "No need, Jeff Tracy. I have asked for Collette's ashes to be brought back here. Tin-Tin and I will mourn her and be on our way."

"Doesn't Collette have family?"

He shook his head. "We were her only family."

Just like Lucy, Jeff thought. "But what about the court date?"

"My brother can have the land. It means nothing to me now."

"What about the workers here?"

"They go from farm to farm during the season. The other farms will take them in."

"Do you have a job?"

"There are many places that would hire me, Jeff Tracy."

"Why not come with me, then? I can get you a job at NASA. The food department is always looking for creative chefs."

He seemed to consider a moment. "Yes. Yes, I will do that, Jeff Tracy. Thank you."

Jeff took a sip of coffee. "Believe me, an astronaut would give a lot to get this kind of food on a mission."

A large crowd gathered at the river. Jeff stood at a distance and watched reverently as Kyrano shook Collette's ashes into the water. Tin-Tin also took a turn. While scanning the assembly, Jeff saw Bela Ghat standing at the edges. He could not help but wonder if Kyrano's half-brother had anything to do with the fire. From what he saw, Kyrano and Collette were simply too conscientious to let incense burn carelessly, and if it were an accident, it was an awfully convenient one for him. Jeff had hinted as such to Kyrano, but Kyrano's response made it clear that he was not interested in pursuing the theory. In a way, Jeff could see the point—it would change nothing, Collette would still be gone.

Afterward, Kyrano, Tin-Tin, and Jeff got into Kyrano's boat to go to the coast. There they would find transportation to Singapore. Kyrano asked if Jeff would drive the boat; the GPS showed their destination. Jeff took the controls as Kyrano sat next to Tin-Tin in the stern, his arm around her, speaking quietly with her. Tin-Tin seemed calmer now, and occasionally smiled during their conversation. As they passed the ruins, Jeff looked up and saw that the jeep was gone; the rental company must have picked it up.

When they got to the coast, Kyrano secured the boat to a slip in a crowded dock. He seemed to know the dock owner, and Jeff guessed the conference at the computer screen and signing of forms was Kyrano selling his boat. Kyrano then led the way to the bus station, where they would pick up a shuttle to Singapore.

When they got to the station, it was packed. People stood virtually shoulder to shoulder.

"Is it rush hour?" Jeff asked, looking at his watch.

"These are travelers," Kyrano said, pointing out the bundles and luggage. He struck up a conversation with the people in front of him in line, then turned to Jeff. "They say that they are from a village, many miles up the coast. There was an old factory there. There was an explosion in the power generator, so they could not work there anymore. They are going to seek work elsewhere."

"Did the explosion happen after work hours?"

"No. Many were hurt."

"I presume the authorities came to help them?"

"Yes, but there would be only one small fire truck and one tiny infirmary in such a remote village. It can take hours for more help to arrive."

Jeff shook his head sadly. So much tragedy. So little help. Someone ought to do something. He had shared these thoughts before, particularly with the guy who worked at the Air Force Base where he had flown experimental jets in his younger days. What was the guy's name again? Tuttle? Yes, Jeremiah had agreed with him, and thought that Jeff was just the person to do it. But how?

The ride to Singapore was relatively brief. At the border, Jeff found that Kyrano had a universal security passport—just as Jeff did—meaning he had undergone a background check and was cleared to go anywhere. Once in Singapore, Jeff took a cab to the timeshare, got his luggage, and checked out. He met Kyrano and Tin-Tin at the airport. At customs, they easily secured a temporary tourist visa for Kyrano and Tin-Tin; Jeff knew that once Kyrano was at NASA, they could secure a work permit for him.

The flight back to the United States was long. He piloted; Kyrano and Tin-Tin sat together in the back. Jeff found himself with plenty of time to think. Advanced rescue equipment, the type which could handle major disasters, did not even exist. It would have to be invented, the technology developed, and that would take money. NASA and its contractors did cutting-edge work, but Jeff needed something still more advanced.

Very well, he would have to do it himself. He would become a contractor. That would give him the freedom to develop the technology, and the excuse to do a talent search. It would also allow him to stay close to home and raise his boys. As for money, he remembered what Lucy's agent—Alice—had said over the phone. Lucy's artwork was now worth a lot of money;

although he hated to give up anything of Lucy's, he knew that Lucy would understand.

His mind made up, he turned to Kyrano and Tin-Tin. "How are you doing?"

"We will heal, Jeff Tracy, we will heal."

Jeff nodded. "And so will I."

3

John Tracy heard the distress call first. At half time, with the score 31-0, he had left the living room with its new wall-sized, 3D-TV, and gone upstairs to the loft in Grandma's house in California to monitor broadcasts. John held licenses in every form of radio communication, and often had conversations with people all around the world. Today, the aircraft frequencies had caught his attention.

He raced downstairs, past Grandma's framed photo of the Tracy nebula that he had discovered in his graduate school research, past the photo of older brother Scott receiving the Distinguished Flying Cross, past the photo of younger brother Alan getting the trophy for his first Grand Prix win, past the photo of his younger brother Gordon receiving the gold medal in the Olympics, past the plaque that Virgil received, commemorating his first place finish in the national piano competition. His father and brothers, hearing him tear down the steps, turned from where they sat on the oversized couch.

"Father," John said breathlessly, "I picked up a mayday from an airliner!"

Scott put an arm on the back of the couch. "Where? When? Which aircraft?"

Jeff Tracy turned in his seat. "Has Air Rescue been notified?"

"Yes," John said, circling the couch so that he could face the rest of his family, "and I picked up chatter between the pilots and air traffic control. They're calling the aircraft engineers. There's something wrong with the hydraulic system."

"What happened?" Virgil asked.

"The pilots heard a loud pop! and the plane started to descend. They regained control through the backup systems, but just barely. They're hoping to make it to Parola Sands airport."

"That's just down the road," Gordon said.

"How many souls on board?" Jeff asked.

"The pilot said 138. It's a modern AC-class jet."

Scott turned to Jeff. "Parola Sands doesn't have the personnel or type of equipment to deal with that kind of emergency, Father."

Jeff turned to John. "How far are they away?"

"At current speed, a little over an hour."

"Air Rescue could barely make it from their nearest station by that time," Virgil pointed out.

"It could take up to an hour just to call the rescue squad to the planes and get them in the air," Scott pointed out.

"We could help," Alan said.

"How about it, Father," Scott said. "We've all had paramedic training when we served as volunteer firefighters in Kansas. You, me, and Gordon have had additional rescue training in the service."

Jeff stood and faced his sons. All now were strapping young men. Scott, at six foot two, took after him the most with the dark brown hair that Jeff had had at thirty. Virgil, at six foot even, most resembled Lucy in face and temperament, despite his large muscular build. John equaled Scott at six foot two, but had a slim frame and blond—almost white—hair that curled in the front (the boys called it "the superhero curl"). Gordon at five foot eleven was the slimmest, with reddish-blond hair. Alan at six foot one sported blond hair and a sturdy frame. Jeff had no doubt they were all equal to any task asked of them.

"What is it, Father?" Scott asked. "You look as if you're about to cross the point of no return."

"Do I?" Jeff asked. "Yes, of course, we have to help. Gather the first aid kits and some extra blankets. Alan will drive the minivan."

"We're going, too," Tin-Tin called.

Jeff turned to the kitchen entrance. Grandma had invited Kyrano and his daughter Tin-Tin to spend Christmas with them at her new house in California. They were Buddhists, but always part of the Tracy Christmases since they moved to the U.S., and they had stayed through New Year's. The two women and Kyrano had looked on while the Tracy men talked about the plane.

"I've completed my paramedic training," Tin-Tin added.

"I will come," Kyrano said. "You will need every pair of hands."

"You're not going to leave me behind!" Grandma insisted.

"Okay!" Jeff said. "Alan, you drive the minivan. Let's move!"

Alan, the professional race car driver, sped down the road toward the airport. He found few cars on the road this holiday afternoon; this part of the desert road was not well-traveled even on regular days. Traffic tended to come and go from the other side of the airport—the road that went to L.A. and San Diego.

"This wasn't on the half-time news," Scott said, "so we shouldn't run into people driving to the airport to watch the plane come in."

"The news services haven't covered a plane in flight in distress since the Mobile crash six years ago," Virgil observed.

"Yeah, you don't want a plane crashing right on the curiosity-seekers," Gordon said.

"Where's the plane coming from, John?" Alan asked, keeping an eye on the road and the speedometer. All they needed now was an automated speed monitor calling a patrol car to pull them over.

"East northeast," John said, looking out the window in that direction.

"Okay, I'll park the van on the access road parallel to the east runway."

The access road was little more than a gravel path next to the airport. They had used it mostly to get to their private hangar where Jeff's personal jet currently rested. Alan drove off the gravel into the flat sand next to the road and stopped the car. Everyone got out.

John put on a headset and pulled out his oversized binoculars, generally used for casual stargazing. Meanwhile, Jeff scanned the airport with his power binoculars.

"They've got fire trucks and ambulances parked near the runway," Jeff said.

John put a hand to his headphones. "The pilot just radioed that he thinks he can make it to the runway." He raised the binoculars to his eyes and scanned east-northeast. He put them down and pointed. "There it is."

A tiny, sleek plane in the distance grew larger by the second.

"No smoke," Scott said. "It must be an internal problem."

"Landing gear coming in place," Jeff said, looking through his binoculars. "No problem there."

Virgil also had binoculars. "Flaps aren't in position."

"Yeah," Scott said. "It's rocking back and forth."

"They're probably having trouble keeping it under control," Alan said.

Now that the plane was in clear view, they could plainly see that the pilots were struggling to keep it on a steady course.

"It looks like it's trying to tumble," Tin-Tin observed.

"I'm wondering what I would do," Virgil said, and the rest of them mumbled agreement. All the Tracy brothers, and Tin-Tin, had learned how to fly planes before learning how to drive cars. The brothers, in addition, had all taken astronaut training.

For a breathtaking minute, it seemed as if the plane would make the runway. Scott, Virgil, and John made hand motions as if they could push the air around the plane to make it descend safely.

"Come on, baby," Jeff muttered.

Suddenly, the plane dipped off the path, nose first, and struck the ground. They heard a sickening crunch before the plane split into three pieces.

"Into the van," Jeff shouted.

They crowded in. The minivan bumped along the desert flat toward the plane. From the side windows, they could see the ambulance and fire trucks converging.

"The fuel tank had to be nearly empty," Jeff observed. "No fire."

Alan stopped the van a distance away. They piled out of the minivan and opened the back doors, grabbing first aid kits and blankets. Running to the plane, they met passengers already stumbling out of the wreckage.

"Anyone hurt?" Jeff called, and the rest of his party repeated the call. Almost immediately, they were answered with "Over here!" or "Help! Help!" They scattered to aid the victims.

A man hurrying from the plane met Alan and John. "Please! My wife! She's wedged in and I can't get her out." The man turned and sprinted back to the plane. Alan and John ran after him. This was the middle section, and when they stepped inside on one end, they could see out the other end. In between lay a wreck of twisted and broken seats, and debris from the overhead compartments. People groaned and writhed in what was left of their seats. Alan heard a small boy's voice crying, "Mommy, Mommy!" He and John paused and exchanged a look. "I'll get him," Alan said. John nodded and followed the man.

Making his way around the debris, Alan came to a little boy patting the back of a limp woman leaning forward in the seat, head down, held only in place by the seat belt. The boy turned to Alan. "Mommy won't wake up!"

Alan checked the woman's vital signs, but could tell even before he did that Mommy was not going to wake up. "Come on," he said to the boy, and picked him up.

"No!" screamed the boy. "Mommy! I want my Mommy!" He kicked and struggled in Alan's arms. Alan approached a woman in a firefighter's uniform and handed her the boy. He pointed. "His mother's over there," he said softly. "She didn't make it."

"Are you all right?" she said, addressing Alan.

"Yes, I'm not a passenger."

"Then you shouldn't be here," the firefighter said.

"I came to help. I'm a certified paramedic."

"Then you should have a paramedic's badge or something."

Alan had no answer. He walked away, using his palm to wipe his wet face. It was too much like when he had lost his own mother.

Meanwhile, Scott checked the flight crew. Within minutes, he determined that pilot, co-pilot, and navigator had all perished. A uniformed airport security officer poked his head in what was left of the cockpit. "All dead," Scott said to him, sadly. "They gave their lives to try to save the passengers."

The officer nodded. "You okay, buddy?"

"Yes. I'm an Air Force captain on leave just near here. I came to see if I could help."

"You should have put your uniform on before coming here," the officer said. "We don't need civilians poking around."

"Right now, you need all the help you can get!" Scott protested, and walked past the officer before he really lost his temper.

Countdown to Action! 45

Once the professional first responders realized that the Tracys and Kyranos knew what they were doing and not getting in the way, they allowed them to stay on and render aid. Air Rescue arrived in helijets just as the last of the passengers—live, injured, or dead—were being taken away. The Federal National Transportation Safety Board crash investigators took statements and then sent the first responders away.

They all went back to the minivan, silently. Alan started the van and proceeded up the road. Airport security directed them around the media trucks and gawkers who had shown up since the crash. No one said anything on the ride back, or when they came in the house. All of their clothes had been stained with the blood or vomit of the victims. The two ladies retired to the upstairs showers; the men lined up at the downstairs facilities.

Alan absent-mindedly flipped on the TV. "...earlier this afternoon, we watched the greatest comeback in football history," the announcer proclaimed with glee, "42 to 34, the final score!"

The Tracy men stared at the screen as if the announcer was from Mars.

As they emerged from the shower, the Tracy men again plopped onto the couch wearing their bathrobes, toweling their hair. With the football festivities over, the station played a movie: *It's A Wonderful Life*. They watched the film silently as Kyrano padded into the kitchen. Jeff tried to wave him over, but Kyrano waved a friendly, if weary, negation.

"If I knew how to cook, I'd join him just to take my mind off...," Virgil said, the first words spoken since they had returned. The others simply nodded.

Kyrano softly announced supper, and they all took their usual places around the kitchen table. Tin-Tin sat by her father, her hair wrapped in a towel. Grandma's damp hair hung limp. They ate without conversation, speaking only to ask for the coffee or a dish to be passed. The tinkling clash of silverware with plates filled the void.

"Another great meal, Kyrano," Jeff said softly as he pushed his plate aside; the others murmured agreement. They all helped clear the table and stack the dishes in the washer; then they sat again while Grandma proudly dished out the apple pie.

"You know, Dad," Scott said between bites, "it ought to be possible now to design a vehicle which can help in these kinds of situations."

"Yeah," Virgil said, "Tracy Technologies has the means. If we can build moon vehicles and shelters, we ought to be able to design heavy-duty machinery for use right here on Earth."

"That guy that I was with in astronaut training could do it," John interjected. "He was always sketching aircraft designs in class. They were pretty astounding."

"What did you say everyone called him?" Gordon asked. "Brains?"

"Didn't you hire him, Father?" Alan asked.

Jeff nodded.

Scott held out his arm and let his forearm dangle at a 90 degree angle. "You could design an aircraft with some sort of giant clamps and grab the airplane in mid-air." He demonstrated by clasping his other arm with the dangling hand.

Jeff watched Scott without comment.

"It's not as easy as just designing a new aircraft," Tin-Tin said. "There would have to be a base to store it in, and then trained personnel to fly and maintain it...."

"Gee, you'd have to put one of those at every air rescue station on the planet," Alan said.

"There would have to be security," Scott added. "If it got into the wrong hands, a madman could just pluck planes from the sky at will."

"I still think we could do it," John said. "Think of the lives we could save."

"What about it, Father?" Virgil asked.

The corners of Jeff's mouth twitched, as if he had been suppressing a smile. He got up without a word, went into the living room, and came back with a laptop. Pushing his pie plate aside, he set it on the table. He keyed in the combination to open the laptop, then pressed his thumb on the identity square. The screen came to life.

The Tracy sons crowded around. Squeezing together so they could all view the screen required a team effort, but they were practiced at it.

Jeff typed in his password. "Ever since your mother died, I've been thinking the same thing you have just now...that the

Countdown to Action! 47

technology has to be available to save people in impossible situations. So I've been discreetly asking some questions, and this is what I've come up with."

A picture of what seemed to be a giant missile came on the screen, along with diagrams. "This is a rocket reconnaissance vehicle. Piloted by one man, it can reach anywhere on the planet in 2 hours or less, at a top speed of 15,000 miles per hour...."

"Fifteen *thousand*?" Scott blurted out.

"How is that even possible?" Alan said.

Jeff gestured at John. "That young man John went to Tracy College with has designed this and the other vehicles we would need."

"What others?" Virgil said eagerly.

Jeff pressed another button on the laptop. A huge, beetle-shaped aircraft came into view. "This would be for heavy rescue." He pointed to the screen. "The center is a removable pod. The pods can carry rescue equipment. Using several pods, we can store different kinds of machinery, and pick up the pod needed for each individual situation, ready to go."

"Wow," Virgil said, smiling. He patted John on the back companionably.

"This," Jeff indicated the screen as it changed again, "is a spacecraft we can use for space emergencies."

"Boy, that's overdue!" John said.

"Yeah," Alan said. "No government has much of anything for space rescues."

"And this," Jeff continued, "is a submarine. It can be carried in one of the pods and transported anywhere on earth on the heavy rescue craft."

"How fast can the heavy rescue craft go?" Virgil asked. "It can't go as fast as the first one."

"No, but Brains thinks it can reach 12,000 miles per hour," Jeff replied.

Virgil whistled in appreciation.

Gordon reached over to touch the screen, as if fondling the underwater craft. "The basic concept is fine, but I think I'd want to make some modifications."

"I was hoping you would," Jeff said, turning to him. Facing the screen, he said, "And the last piece of basic equipment...

a satellite station. We need satellite communication, GPS, and space surveillance in order to coordinate everything."

"Yeah, but will International Space Control let us put this kind of satellite in space?" John asked.

"Tracy Technologies has already been granted the permit," Jeff said.

"Really?" Alan said, impressed.

"But what they're going to put up is an ordinary communications satellite," Jeff added. "Once it's up, we'll use our new space vehicle to go up and add our own modifications."

Scott turned to John. "This is looking better all the time."

John put a finger on the screen, right at the center of the proposed satellite. "Dad, if you're going to put something in space of that size, you've *got* to add an observatory. It won't be hard, you have to get the optical equipment for earth surveillance anyway—just order an extra set so I can point it out to space."

Jeff craned his neck so he could look at his middle son. "Are you volunteering to operate the station?"

"I...I guess I am."

"Hey, I want to get in on this, too!" Alan said.

Jeff turned to his youngest son. "That's good, because we need two people to work in one-month shifts."

"Does that mean I get the observatory?" John asked.

Jeff chuckled and turned back to the screen. "I'll have Brains get right on it. And, I'll double the order on the optics."

"Do we draw straws for the others?" Scott asked.

Jeff glanced up at his eldest son. "We're getting a little ahead of ourselves. First, let's all sit down." He gestured, and his five sons took their seats. Jeff shut the laptop. Tin-Tin, Grandma, and Kyrano, who had been looking on during the discussion, also sat.

Folding his hands on the table, Jeff looked at his sons. "Before we go any further on this, I want you boys to know what you're getting into. You're all of the age where men usually want to start settling down. By the time I was Scott's age, four of you boys were already born. If you sign on to this, you'll have to put any plans to start a family aside, at least for the first couple of years while we're establishing ourselves."

Countdown to Action!

"If?" Alan asked. "You mean we have a choice?"

"Of course you do! I'm going to be asking a lot of you, and it's not going to work if you feel you're being forced." Jeff nodded to two of his sons. "Scott, Gordon, your current enlistments are almost up. You'd have to leave your respective services."

Gordon and Scott looked at each other, but said nothing.

"Alan, you'll have to retire from race car driving, for the time being."

"Can't I just go back and forth?"

"No, Alan, you'll be far too busy, at least in the first year. And it's not fair to your pit crew...they'll need to find work elsewhere. The Parola Sands race this Saturday will have to be your last for a while...maybe a long while."

Alan sighed, and leaned back in his chair, frowning.

Scott leaned toward him and said in a low voice, "Think of the spaceship, Alan."

Alan's face brightened immediately.

"Virgil, John, you'd have to give up your jobs at Tracy Technologies, and John, that also means giving up your guest lecturer position in the astronomy department at NYU."

"Are you leaving Tracy Technologies, Father?" Virgil asked.

"Yes, I'm planning a public statement that I'm retiring from the day-to-day running of the company. I'll still have a toe in the water, so to speak, but once I make my announcement, I won't be much more than a figurehead. I've been grooming my replacements for years; the company will be in good hands. International Rescue will require my total commitment, and yours, if you choose to join."

"International Rescue?" Scott said. "Is that what we're calling it?"

"Yes. Let me add that you'll all be provided for. You'll be working hard, risking your lives...."

"Not too much, I hope," Grandma interjected.

Jeff turned to her. "Not any more, or any less, than when they worked as volunteer firefighters, or when Gordon spent a year at the bottom of the ocean, or when Scott test piloted the latest supersonic jets for the Air Force or when Alan crashed his car at his first Grand Prix."

Alan folded his arms. "You had to remind me of that."

"So we get an allowance," Gordon said with a smile, returning to the previous topic.

Jeff nodded. "Quite a generous one, if I may say so. I'll transfer an annual stipend equivalent to the salary for the president of the U.S."

Virgil whistled.

"...and if you sign on, you'll earn every penny, I guarantee it," Jeff said. "One more thing: I'll always be your father, and I'll always love you, but when you sign on to International Rescue, I want it clear right now that I'll be in charge. We'll consult and discuss, as we always do, but my word will be final, and I expect that when I give a directive, it will be carried out. If you can't agree to this, I'll respect that, but if you're going to be part of the International Rescue team, that's how it's going to be."

The brothers looked silently from one to the other.

"This is a solemn decision, maybe the most important one you'll make in your lives. If you want to sleep on it, think it over for a couple of days, I understand."

"I'm in," Scott said, without hesitation.

"Me, too," Virgil chimed in.

John held up a hand, fingers spread. "Let's see, I get a telescope outside the atmosphere and don't have to sign up for telescope time," he touched an index finger. "I get to fly a rocket ship," he touched another finger. "I get a state-of-the-art communications system," he touched another finger. "And I get to make a positive difference in people's lives," he touched another finger. "Frankly, I'd pay someone for the chance to do all that."

"Sounds like fun," Gordon said.

"You would," Alan said to Gordon.

Gordon turned to him. "Well, are you in or aren't you?"

Alan looked at John. "You're going to have to wrestle me for who gets to fly the rocket ship first."

"Let's not lose our focus," Jeff said. "This isn't about a bunch of flying machines. It's a serious business about saving people's lives, in situations where no one else can come to help."

Gordon slapped the table. "Well, I hope we're allowed to be happy if we save someone from certain death!"

Jeff smiled. "Okay, okay. I get the picture. There's a certain amount of excitement in any kind of rescue work, and we'll undoubtedly have our share of that."

"That's a relief!" Gordon said.

"Is there a place in International Rescue for us?" Tin-Tin asked.

"Of course there is!" Grandma said before Jeff could answer.

Jeff had opened his mouth, but closed it when Grandma replied. When she finished, Jeff turned to the young woman. "There is. But I don't want you to change your plans, Tin-Tin. Finish the work on your engineering degree, go on your European tour, and by that time we should be ready to start our operation."

"But Dad," Scott said, tapping the table with a hand, "this is a massive project. It would have to take years."

"Months," Jeff replied. "The same Tracy Technologies equipment that built the moon base, and the launch facilities at Glen Allyn field, will enable us to build our base, aircraft, and everything else we need. Brains has the plans all laid out in step-by-step detail."

"Are we building our base here?" Scott asked. "Out in the desert?"

"No," Jeff said. "Secrecy will be essential for our operation. We'll have to be as far from civilization as possible."

"Antarctica?" Gordon teased.

Jeff smiled. "No, though I have to admit I thought about it." Alan gasped, and Jeff repeated, "No. Brains and I did some scouting and found an uninhabited island in the South Pacific. Brains did a geological survey and found it would be perfect for our purposes. I bought the island and one nearby. There isn't any other land anywhere for hundreds of miles in any direction."

"How do we get everything out that far?" Scott asked.

"I've rented a barge, everything is on it." He gestured to Gordon. "Gordon, here, can pilot anything that travels on or under the sea. That will be our home while we're constructing everything."

"What about the Tracy yacht?" Alan asked.

"We'll bring that when we're ready to move in with the furniture," Jeff said. "But the barge has 18 rooms for crew; they're comfortable, single-occupancy cabins, even if they're only the size of an average hotel room."

"Won't the people who loaded the barge get a hint of what we're up to by what's on there?" Virgil asked.

Jeff shook his head. "To avoid inspections, most of the items have been transported on Tracy Technologies company jets in coded containers. What we need has come from a dozen different places, and seems to be basic electronic and construction materials. It will only look as if eccentric billionaire Jeff Tracy is building an exotic palace for himself on a tropical island paradise, complete with state-of-the-art technology."

"Gee Dad," John said. "I had no idea that you had been doing all this planning. Did you ever think of telling us before?"

"I wanted to be sure I could do this first," Jeff replied, "and that it wasn't just a crazy idea that couldn't be implemented in a million years. It wasn't until someone told me of this genius with impossible concepts and I went to hear Brains give a lecture in France that I realized International Rescue could become a reality."

"He told me everyone laughed at him," John said.

Jeff nodded. "Everyone but me, that is."

"When do we get started?" Alan asked.

"As soon as you boys can get your affairs together and join me in Hilo at the Tracy Technologies docks. I hope it goes without saying that this is top secret. You will tell no one outside this room, except Brains."

The others nodded.

"Grandma will stay here until everything is constructed and our operation is underway." He turned to Kyrano. "Kyrano, you can come with Tin-Tin when she's back from Europe."

"No," Kyrano said softly. "I will come with you to the island."

"Kyrano," Jeff said kindly, "we need everyone there with engineering experience. All we'll be doing is construction."

"Not all," Kyrano said. "You will need to eat, and wash clothes, and keep things clean."

"We all know how to cook, Kyrano, we've been doing it for years."

"All Virgil knows how to make is a bologna sandwich," Alan said.

Virgil inclined his head in acknowledgment.

"And heating up food in the microwave, maybe," Grandma murmured.

"I can do a little more than that, Mother," Jeff said.

"A little more, yes," Kyrano said. "But forgive me, you do not do cooking work as well as the engineering work. If I come and cook, you will be better nourished, and better able to work. The time you would spend on cooking you can spend on construction. You will feel better and work better if you have clean clothes every day, not wearing the same old sweaty clothes every day until they fall off."

"We know how to do laundry, Kyrano."

"I have known you for many years, Jeff Tracy, and I know that when you and the boys are working on a project, the laundry does not get done."

The Tracy men looked sheepish. Grandma smiled and nodded at Kyrano.

"Kyrano," Jeff said, "you've been the chief food researcher and dietitian at NASA for many years, as well as manager of the Kew Gardens. We can't ask you to give that up just to do our housekeeping."

"You are not asking, Jeff Tracy. I am offering to do this. When I worked at Kew Gardens, I fed people's souls. When I work at NASA, I enable the astronauts to do their jobs. That is important work. I get great satisfaction from it. I cannot do engineering work, as you said, but I can feed your bodies and your souls so that through your work, no one else needs to die unnecessarily. I would consider that an honor."

Jeff found himself speechless for a few moments. Finally, he replied, "What can I say?"

"You can say, 'Kyrano, welcome to International Rescue.'" He stood and brought out the champagne from the wine closet. Grandma, seeing what Kyrano had in mind, handed out the champagne flutes. When they all had a filled glass, Kyrano raised his. "To International Rescue."

"To International Rescue," they all repeated. They clinked their glasses together, and drank.

Scott put his down. "Now the real work begins."

4

"The Colonel is expecting you," said the aide as Scott walked through the outer office. He knocked on the door that had "Colonel Roger Freelander" on the name plate, and entered when he heard "come in." He stepped to the desk where Freelander sat, saluted, and took a seat at Freelander's invitation.

"I have your discharge forms, Captain," Freelander said to Scott, "but I wanted to have a talk with you before I put them through."

"Sir?"

"I saw your Dad's press conference about him retiring, not just from his company, but public life. I hope he's in good health?"

"He's fine, sir."

Freelander nodded. "Good." He gestured at Scott. "And about the part about taking his sons with him...nothing wrong with you or your brothers...no suddenly discovered fatal diseases, anything like that?"

"No sir, we're all fine."

"No scandals, financial problems?"

"No, sir, nothing."

The colonel folded his hands on his desk. "Look, Captain, I know this is all none of my business, but I feel I really need to tell you...when a man gets to your father's age, sometimes he thinks that he's done his part for the world and it's time to take it easy. Nothing wrong with that, of course, but son, you still have a good deal of your life ahead of you. You've had a brilliant career here in the Air Force, and I just think you're making a big mistake in giving it up."

"It's been an honor and a privilege to serve, sir. I've enjoyed every minute of it. But it's time for me to go."

"And do what? Sit in the sun on some tropical island? That's going to get old, pretty fast. You're a man of action, Tracy. That's not the life for you."

"I have other things I want to do, sir."

Freelander smiled. "Anything you want to do, Tracy, we'll match it. You've had astronaut experience. Do you want a post on the moon base? It's yours. You want an assignment on a fast jet? Your father's old friend, Colonel Casey, is working on a rocket engine fighter jet, code named Red Arrow. It'll be the fastest, toughest thing in the skies, and it's yours if you want it. You can't possibly get anything that good in civilian life, nowhere near."

Scott had to hold back a smile. He pressed his lips together. "It does sound good, sir, but...."

Freelander shook his head sadly. He looked right at Scott. "Can I appeal to your sense of morality? There are still a lot of battles to be fought, Tracy, still a lot of madmen out there ready to start a war to get what they want. Hell, Tracy, you not only were instrumental in the Peninsula conflict, we're still trying to figure out how you managed to land your plane right smack in the middle of hostile territory, pick up our wounded, and get back into the air without taking a hit."

This time, Scott did smile.

"You saved a lot of lives that day, Tracy," Freelander continued, "and the Air Force needs men like you to continue saving lives. You know from your own experience that without air superiority, the entire world is at risk."

Scott lowered his head, thinking. Freelander was right. The world depended on safe aviation, now more than any other time in history. Any threat to aviation put lives at stake. Yet, that is why the world needed the machines that his father showed him, and that is why he had to pilot them.

He looked Freelander in the eye. "I'm sorry, sir, but I have to leave. At least for now."

Freelander sighed. He stood, obligating Scott to stand. "All right. But don't stay away too long. The longer you stay out, the harder it will be to come back. I'm hoping you just need a little time to think and reorganize."

Scott felt it better not to respond to that. In a few seconds, Freelander extended his hand. "Good luck, son."

Scott took his hand. "Thank you, sir."

* * *

At Aquanaut Headquarters, Gordon Tracy found Commodore Paul Tschida looking at a computer screen when he walked in. He saluted and held out a datacard. "Lieutenant Tracy, respectfully turning in my discharge, sir."

Tschida looked at him. Then he looked around him. Then he looked back at him. "All right, Tracy, what is it this time?"

"Sir?"

"Come on, what did you do? Let me guess...you've got four of your buddies lined up outside, and you'll each come in and give me your fake discharge cards, and then when I put them in the computer, the screen will erupt with talking mermaid pop-ups."

"No, sir, there's no one but me, and these are my real discharge forms."

"You expect me to believe that? Gordon Tracy, who would grow gills if it were possible, leaving the aquanaut corps?"

"It's true, sir. Here." He handed Tschida the card.

The Commodore took it gingerly between a thumb and forefinger. "This isn't a replica made of sugar that's going to crumble in 20 seconds, is it?"

"No, sir."

Slowly, with a skeptical expression, Tschida put the card into the computer, and read the screen. His eyebrows went up. He turned back to Gordon. "Okay, now, level with me, Tracy. What's behind this? If you're turning in your discharge, it has to be something more than when you gave the aquanaut swim team suits that dissolved in water, or dumped the octopus into the officers' swimming pool...," he snapped his fingers, "...oh, yeah, after you drained it and put in sea water...," he made quotation marks with his fingers, "'so the octopus would feel right at home.'"

"I'm not in any trouble, sir."

He gestured to the computer screen. "You know what this means, don't you? You're gone, done."

"Yes, sir."

"No coming back."

"Yes, sir."

He waved at the open doorway. "You can't just walk out the door, come back in 2 minutes later, and tell me you were just kidding."

"I understand that, sir."

"Well, I don't understand you, Tracy. You understand that?"

Gordon took a moment to analyze. "I...think so, sir."

"You better do more than think, lieutenant. You better know. You're only 22 years old! You're throwing your life away!"

"I've thought it out, sir."

"No, I don't think you have. Where are you going to go?"

"To an island in the South Pacific, sir. Plenty of water there."

"You mean with your Dad? I saw that press conference. I thought 'sons' meant his civilian sons. You mean your eldest brother, Captain Scott Tracy, USAF, is going along, too?"

"We're all going, sir."

Tschida sat back for a moment, agape. Then he straightened in his chair. "Tracy, I don't know what your father said to get you and your brothers to take off to the middle of nowhere, but mark my words, if you leave the service here, you'll regret it for the rest of your life."

"I've made up my mind, sir."

"What are you going to do, Tracy? Seriously, what are you going to do?"

"I'm going to have fun, sir," Gordon said with a straight face.

Tschida drummed the desk with his fingertips. He took a breath. "All right. I'll put through the discharge."

"Thank you, sir."

Tschida turned to the computer. "You can go."

"It's been a pleasure, sir."

"Oh, I know it has."

Gordon saluted. Tschida returned the salute; Gordon walked out, pulling out the keycard to his car. When he got to the car, he felt for his wallet and found it had slipped out. He walked back to just outside Tschida's office and picked it up. The door was open.

"I don't know whether to be happy or annoyed," Tschida's voice said.

"Sir?" asked his aide.

"On one hand, I'm relieved we don't have to put up with any more of Tracy's practical jokes. On the other hand, he was the best of the aquanaut corps and I'm sorry to lose him."

Gordon smiled and silently padded back to his car.

* * *

John Tracy took his usual morning run in Central Park. At the end of his run, he entered the Freedom Tower, where Tracy Technologies had its New York headquarters on the 52nd through 54th floors. He used the company showers just off the company gym and dressed in his business suit. His office, just down the hall, had "Office of the Comptroller" above the name plate. He packed his things, and last of all, slid off the name plate. Sighing, he turned to the Associate Comptroller, whose desk was just outside.

"Well, Maribeth, the office is yours, now."

"I'll sure miss you, John," she said.

He nodded.

"And not just at the office. The nights at the opera, the walks in Central Park...Miller over in accounting isn't nearly as much fun."

He chuckled. "I'll miss you, too." When his father said that they would have to give up family life, he had not fully realized what that meant...until now.

She met his eye. "Are you giving up the lecturer post, too?"

John nodded. "Yes. I have to stop at NYU. I just came here to pack up my things."

"I'll see that they're shipped to your address in Hilo."

"Thanks." He wanted to say more, but there was really nothing more to say. He had broken the news to her last night at the restaurant, and they agreed that they were just friends and co-workers, and it had been fine, and they really had not expected anything more to develop...or had they? Still, they had never slept together, never flirted in the office...yes, they were just friends. But they would miss each other, just the same, and lingering now would simply prolong the sadness they both felt. He exchanged a parting smile with her, and turned to walk out the door.

Carl Swenson, head of the physical science departments at NYU, could be mistaken for Albert Einstein at a distance—mostly due to the unkempt shock of white hair. While similar to Einstein in intellect, there was no resemblance when it came to temperament, which John found when he turned in his resignation.

"What?" Swenson exclaimed, staring at the PDA screen that John handed him.

"My term as lecturer was over anyway. It's the end of the semester and I've turned in the final grades of my students."

"You can't do this! John...John, this was going to be a surprise, but I went to the faculty council and we were going to offer you a tenure-track position in the astronomy department!"

John turned to Swenson in wide-eyed astonishment. "I...I didn't know."

"Well, you did know that we've been expanding the science departments at NYU these past 30 years. We were going to have a world-class astronomy department. We're partnering with M.I.T. and Harvard to build a space observatory. With your astronaut training, you'd be the resident astronomer there."

"Oh, wow."

"Yes, wow. So I can't accept your resignation." He handed back the PDA.

John took it, stared at it for a few moments, and put it back on Swenson's desk. "It's a very generous offer...."

"Yes, yes, it is! And you can't turn it down!" he said desperately.

"I'm afraid I have to."

Swenson tore at his hair. "John, John, you're killing me! This is a once-in-a-lifetime opportunity! You won't get a better offer anywhere, at any university, I don't care where you go!"

John pressed his lips together, and inclined his head. "You're right, I won't get a better offer..."

"Then you'll take it!"

"No," John said slowly. "I'm going to go with my Dad...."

"Your Dad! If your Dad jumped off a bridge, would you jump off a bridge, too?"

John chuckled. "I guess I didn't see it quite that way."

"Good! Then you're staying!"

John took a breath. He shook his head.

"John, don't do this! If you don't take this offer, they'll give it to Gilchrist!"

"She's a fine astronomer."

"Fine astronomer, yes! But the point is, if you say no, the offer's gone forever! The faculty council needs the position filled this week...today! And it won't be repeated!"

John reached over and put a hand on Swenson's shoulder. "It's not personal, Professor. It's...business."

Swenson threw up his hands and exhaled explosively. "Business, he says."

John smiled at him. "Thanks for everything. You don't know how much it means to me that you recommended me."

"You don't know how much it means to me that you're leaving." He was almost pouting.

"I'm sorry, Professor."

"It's going to hurt you more than it's hurting me, I guarantee that!"

John took Swenson's hand and shook it. "Goodbye Professor. And I wish you the best with your expansion."

"Well, good luck to you, and I hope you know what you're doing!"

"I do, Professor, I do."

Swenson did not even look at John as John left the office. He simply sat on the edge of his desk, shaking his head.

At the main offices of Tracy Technologies, just outside Kansas City, Virgil Tracy drove up to the guard post at the main gate. The guard waved him through, and he parked outside the engineering building. He saw only a handful of other cars in the lot; as chief engineer—at least he was until noon that day—he had given everyone the day off following his going-away party the night before. As he walked to his office to gather his last remaining personal items, he saw Draper and Beasley in the assembly area through the observation windows. After stuffing his personal belongings in his bag, he shouldered the strap and strode down to the floor to see what was going on.

The two men hovered over the new lunar vehicle, just finished the previous day. "Hi, fellas," he said. "What's up?"

They turned to him. "Hey, Virgil, great party last night," Beasley said.

"Yeah, you play a hot piano," Draper added. "I hope Nelson didn't scratch it when she danced on top of it."

"Naw, it's fine," Virgil said. "The movers are packing it up as we speak." He gestured to the vehicle. "What's the problem?"

The junior engineers turned back to it. "We can't get it to start," Beasley said.

"Ignition disconnect?" Virgil asked.

Draper shook his head. "Checked that."

Virgil put down his bag. "Okay, lets check the specs."

They all walked to the nearest computer terminal and brought up the screens. Virgil pressed some keys; the readout showed which manufacturer provided which part. He tapped the screen with the nail of his index finger. "There it is."

"What?" Draper asked.

Virgil turned to him. "The ignition system was made by Janis Industries."

Draper put a hand on a hip. "Yeah, but what does that have to do with it not starting?"

"Everything we get from Janus has to be altered to meet our specifications. It says so right," Virgil clicked the mouse on the part, "here."

"Oops," Draper said.

"That should have been done before it got to you. Someone missed it. Tell Nelson; she'll track it down and talk to the one who should have done it. Probably just a new hire."

Beasley sighed and smiled. "Don't know what we'll do without you, Virgil."

He smiled back. "You'll do just fine."

Alan Tracy crossed the finish line at the Parola Sands Grand Prix and drove his car to the winner's circle. After taking off his helmet and disconnecting all the safety restraints, he climbed out of the car and met the racing officials, who handed him his trophy. He posed for the photographers as the reporters asked him questions.

"Now that you've graduated from college, Tracy, I presume you'll be entering even more races?"

"No, actually, I'm going to take it easy for a while." He heard groans and exclamations of surprise. "My Dad's going to build a house on an island in the Pacific, and my brothers and I are going to help. So I haven't scheduled any more races." He dismissed the rest of the questions with a wave and a smile, then helped his chief mechanic, Kenny Malone, to get the car back to the garage. The others in his pit crew, Esther Rappaport and Hector Montoya, joined them.

"I sure hate leaving you guys like this," Alan said.

"Oh, we'll be okay," Rappaport said. "We've had lots of offers."

"Yeah, Victor Gomez was around before you arrived," Montoya said, frowning. He exchanged disapproving glances with the other mechanics.

"Why not work for Gomez?" Alan asked. "He's a good driver. He came in right behind me."

"It's not really him," Montoya complained. "It's his new manager, Johnny Gillespie."

"What about him?" Alan asked.

"He does tend to fly off the handle," Malone said.

"Yeah, it's 'my way or the highway' with him," Montoya added.

Before they could discuss Gomez and Gillespie further, they heard a voice from the entrance. "Hey, Alan, great race."

Alan turned. "Brian! Say, you almost passed me on the number three turn."

Brian Vang smiled. "Now that you're leaving the field, the rest of us can win some races for a change." Alan chuckled, and he added, "So I've come to hire your mechanics before someone else does."

"I'd be happy to work for you, Brian," Rappaport said.

"Me, too," Montoya chimed in.

Vang turned to Malone. "How about you, Kenny?"

He grinned and shook his head. "I'm taking some time off, too. My parents are headed off to Australia for six months. I'm going to occupy their house while they're gone. It's right on the beach just south of Tampa Bay. I'm heading for some fun in the sun."

"Well, if you ever get bored, look me up," Vang replied.

Malone nodded.

"It won't be the same around the circuit without you, Alan," Vang said.

"Oh, I'll be around. My grandma lives just down the road. You may see me again some time."

The groundskeeper waved at Jeff as he got out of his car. "Hello, Mr. Tracy. Come to visit the Mrs.?"

Jeff nodded.

Countdown to Action! 63

The man pointed. "She's got more flowers than anyone else here. Fresh ones every week. And I keep the silk arrangements dusted."

"Thank you." Jeff glanced to the side as he went up the walk. He recognized Scott's motorcycle, John's sensible compact electric car, Alan's sportscar, Virgil's convertible, and Gordon's DeLorean-style wing-door car.

When he reached the building, he placed his passcard in the slot next to the door. The door slid open. At the other end of the room, he saw his sons gathered around the flowers.

Scott turned to him. "We had to say goodbye to Mom."

Jeff strode forward and put his hand on Scott's shoulder. "Your mother will always be with us, wherever we go."

Although the mausoleum's vaults were fashioned from cold marble, the flower arrangements added a warm touch. Through the blossoms, Jeff could make out the inscription "Beloved Wife and Mother."

As if by arrangement, each of the Tracy sons, in turn, placed the palm of his hand against the vault, said, "I love you, Mom," gave his father a hug, and left. When they were gone, Jeff, too, placed his hand against the stone. "Well, Lucy, we're finally ready to start. If we succeed, no one will have to lose a loved one again because there's no one who can come to save them. Our boys are the best; I know they can do it, and more. But I have to be honest with you--it means putting our boys in harm's way. That wasn't easy for me to do, but you always said that life is never easy, so I know you understand. I promise I'll do everything I can to keep them safe. I need you to watch over them, too, as you always have. You and I and the boys are a team, and you're the first, best, part." He closed his eyes briefly and took a breath. "I have to go now, Angel. Remember, I love you with all my heart." He briefly put his lips to the marble, caressed the inscription with his fingers, and reluctantly turned away.

5

Gordon Tracy felt in his element, standing on the docks at Hilo, in his captain's uniform. The feel of the boards under his feet, the tang of the salt air, the warm sea breeze, all invigorated him. The giant barge floated at his back as he faced the shoreline, watching as the workers—all bonded Tracy Technologies employees—brought supplies to him and past him onto the vessel. They would stop when they reached him; he would inspect the cargo and check it off on the pocket-sized computer manifest.

None of the other Tracys had boarded yet, but soon he saw Scott coming toward him. His eldest brother pushed a flat, wheeled cart with his luggage, including his guitar. Although he wore civilian clothes, Scott stopped when he drew even with Gordon and saluted. "Permission to come aboard, sir!"

Gordon smiled and returned the salute. "Permission granted, Scott." He brought up another screen on the hand-held computer. "You're in compartment five."

Scott looked over Gordon's arm to see a schematic of the ship. "Okay. I'll settle in."

At that moment, a heavy-set man wearing a uniform identifying him as coming from a local nursery drove up in a motorized cart. On the flat bed of the cart three enormous boxes, each 5 meters long, had been stacked. Alongside of the boxes stood a small potted leafy plant, perhaps 2 meters tall, the sort that would look inconspicuous in an office corner. The nursery man braked the cart when he reached Gordon and climbed out of the driver's seat. He handed Gordon a paper. "Your plants, Mack."

Gordon looked at it curiously. "Well, I did order this," he indicated the office plant, "but I didn't order the others."

"What is it?" Scott asked.

"It says three dozen artificial palm trees." Gordon stepped over to the cart and opened the top box. Inside, as the paper specified, he saw artificial palm trees, ready for assembly.

"That's right, Mack," said the man. "I was told to include those."

"But I'm sure I didn't order these," Gordon protested again.

"I don't think Dad would go for one of your jokes, Gordon." Scott said.

"But Scott, I really didn't order these."

"No. I did," said a voice.

Gordon and Scott turned to see their father standing there, pushing a rolling luggage case.

"Well, I'm glad someone knows what's going on!" said the nursery worker.

Jeff opened a side panel on each box and inspected the cargo. Then he turned to his son. "Let the man through, Gordon."

"Okay, Dad." Gordon added the palms to the manifest and waved the man through.

"What are the palms for?" Scott asked.

Jeff chuckled. "You'll see." He snapped to attention in front of Gordon and saluted smartly. "Permission to come aboard, sir!"

Gordon saluted back. "Permission granted, Dad."

Jeff looked over Gordon's captain's hat, tailored uniform, knee-length khaki pants, knee-length white socks, and white sea shoes. He nodded approvingly, then turned to Scott. "You'll find your uniform on your bed."

"Uniform? You mean we have to wear uniforms?"

They turned to see Alan standing there with a cart like Scott's. Behind him was Virgil with a similar cart carrying his electronic keyboard along with his bags, and John, who had added his Dobsonian telescope to his luggage.

Jeff looked at his youngest son. "Yes, we're all wearing uniforms. We're the only crew on this barge. We're all going to have our individual duties, and we're going to be professionally dressed when on duty."

Alan frowned, but Virgil said, "Good. That means I won't get grease on my favorite shorts."

Jeff let go of his luggage case and walked to the end of the dock, meeting Kyrano and another young man, each of whom pushed his own luggage cart. The others watched as Jeff came forward with the newcomer, who had short dark hair, a high forehead, and large thick glasses.

"Boys, this is Brains. You already know John," Jeff continued, and made the other introductions.

When Alan shook his hand, he said, "Is that what you want us to call you...Brains?"

The young man nodded.

"Do you have another name?" Alan added.

"Just B-b-brains," the young man stuttered.

"Okay, if that's what you want," Alan said amiably.

Jeff took his luggage again and touched Scott's arm. "Scott and I already have permission to go aboard. The rest of you need to ask," he added pointedly.

Once the barge had left the dock, they all assembled in the control room. Gordon proudly explained all the controls. "It's pretty much like a plane on autopilot," he said. "But we do need someone here monitoring at all times."

Alan stood with his arms crossed in front of him. "Why, if it's automatic?"

"Because machines aren't infallible," Jeff explained.

Gordon touched a small metal box clipped to his belt. "If there's any trouble, just page me."

Jeff took his own communications device from his belt and showed the others how to use it before reattaching it.

Kyrano, who had also come for the orientation wearing his chef's uniform, turned to leave.

Alan called to him. "Say, Kyrano, your degree's in botany. What sort of plant is that?" He indicated Gordon's office plant.

Kyrano examined the plant. He put a hand out and fondled a leaf. Smiling, he winked at Gordon and turned to Alan. "Oh, this plant is one of a kind." He walked out the door.

"All right, so don't tell me," Alan complained.

"Alan." Scott pointed to a metal plate on the ceramic pot. "It says 'Ficus' right there."

Alan bent, looked, and shrugged. "I guess it was an obvious question."

Jeff put a hand on John's shoulder. "John, you had a hand in the construction of the moon base, so you already know what Virgil and I need to tell the other boys. You take the first watch here."

"Okay, Dad."

Jeff handed John a data card and pointed to the computer console on top of the control panel. "You can take a look at the schematics while I'm going over them with the others in the cargo hold."

John smiled. "Thanks, Dad."

Jeff led them below decks and gave them a tour though the cargo holds. "All the crew quarters are above deck; this is entirely supplies."

Scott peered through a door as he passed it. "Say, this is a hangar for a helijet."

"We'll need to go to the mainland from time to time, and we can't use a plane until we've built a runway on the island."

"Speaking of which, Dad," Gordon interjected as they continued to walk along, "I signed up for a charity event in Honolulu some time ago. I hope I can still make it."

Jeff turned to him briefly without breaking stride. "When is it?"

"In about a month. We ought to be settled at Tracy Island by then."

"What's involved?" Jeff asked.

"Oh, just a typical water show. Nothing I haven't done a million times before."

"Yeah, like power boat racing," Alan chimed in.

"You know, Gordon," Jeff said, glancing back every so often as he continued to lead the way, "if anything happens to you, we'll be short a man."

"I was counting on you to help with the s-s-submarine," Brains said.

"I'll do all that," Gordon said.

"Let me think about it," Jeff said.

"Okay, Dad," Gordon sounded confident that his father would come around eventually.

Jeff stepped through a door and activated the lights. The other men, as they came through, saw a large, high-ceilinged room. A desk with a computer console stood in a corner near the entrance. Jeff sat and inserted his datacard into the computer. "Come look at this."

The others crowded around. "Our first task will be to create the structures we need to house the equipment," Jeff explained. "That won't be too different from our work at the moon base where we built living quarters and launch pads."

"What about the spaceship and the other aircraft?" Alan asked.

"P-p-patience, Alan," Brains said. "All in good time."

"We can start building some of what we need right here on the barge," Jeff continued. "One of the structures we will need right away is the power plant. Brains, here, has a designed a fusion reactor."

Scott whistled appreciatively. "The only working reactors I know of are experimental ones, in labs."

"I've overcome the p-p-practical problems," Brains said. "All the aircraft will have fusion engines, too."

"Also high on the priority list are the water and sewage treatment plants."

Alan made a face, but said nothing.

"Those were essential structures on the moon base," Virgil assured his younger brother.

"Water is essential to our operation," Brains explained. "We need it to get h-h-hydrogen for the fusion reactors, and oxygen for the spacecraft."

Virgil gathered some of the equipment nearby. As if on cue, he started a lesson. "The key to all this is what we call the 'Tracy weld.' Once we fuse panels in this way, they're as strong as if they were cast in one piece."

"Why not just cast them in one piece?" Alan asked.

"It's hard to transport an entire building in one piece, Alan," Virgil said. "But smaller pieces can be stacked and shipped in compact containers. Plus we get the flexibility to make a number of forms, or alter the plans for the original form."

"Virgil will show you how to do it," Jeff said. "He, John, and I will inspect your work. You'll find that everything we're building is in modular units. Various Tracy Technologies plants have assembled the modules, and we will put them together according to plan." He pointed at the computer screen, which showed the pieces and how they fit together.

Scott rubbed his hands together. "Okay, let's get started."

* * *

Countdown to Action! 69

As Alan sat in the captain's chair on the bridge, he wondered how the last 24 hours had gone so badly. He had awakened in a comfortable hotel in Hilo the day before, excited and ready to get started on building those great airships that his father had talked about during the holidays, only to end up welding bits and pieces of what would become a sewage treatment unit! And even when he did, not one of them passed inspection. His father had reprimanded him, telling him that he had wasted time and materials and that everything he put together would have to be done over. Worse than that, his brothers had not been the least sympathetic—Scott had said that if the sewage plant ever broke, he would make sure that Alan would have to wade through the muck to fix it!

He reached under his collar to scratch his neck. The uniform was another reminder of how awful the day had been. Sure, Alan had agreed that he would follow his father's directives, but he had thought that this would be sort of like his days as a teenager in the Civil Air Patrol, where the supervising adults reminded him of friendly Scout patrol leaders. He had not imagined his father taking the role of a drill sergeant—if he had wanted to join a military organization, he would have enlisted, as Scott and Gordon had.

Now here he was, taking the 0200 to 0600 bridge watch that his father had ordered, after sending him to bed at 2000 hours. Alan had feebly protested that Gordon was the captain of the barge, but Gordon affirmed that Dad was first mate and therefore made crew assignments. There was nothing to look at but the readouts, and although he could see the ocean on the night-vision screen, nothing there had changed for hours. With the monotony of the routine, and the melodious hum of the barge engines, he found himself nodding a couple of times. He would get up, walk around, and drink some coffee—fortunately Kyrano had kept the bridge well supplied—then settle back in the captain's chair.

I'M THIRSTY! bellowed a loud bass voice.

Alan fell out of the chair, heart racing. He looked around to see who had spoken. He got to his feet and checked the communication console. It had not been recently activated; besides, the sound seemed to have come behind him.

I'M THIRSTY!

This time, less startled, Alan turned toward the sound. It seemed to come from the plant. Cautiously, he inched toward it.

I'M THIRSTY, THIRSTY, THIRSTY! The leaves rustled when the voice spoke.

Alan let out a breath. Another of Gordon's practical jokes. He checked the plant thoroughly, but could not find the speaker. It had to be a tiny sound chip, which could be anywhere, and which he probably could not find without a scanner.

THIRSTY!

Alan went to the beverage stand, filled a cup of water, and tossed it into the planter.

THANK YOU squeaked the plant.

Alan sighed and sat down. Yes, it had been a bad 24 hours.

Scott came in exactly at 0600. He jerked a thumb toward the door. "Go get breakfast, Alan."

Alan stood and waved to the plant. "Gordon's wired the plant. It complains that it's thirsty."

Scott glanced at the plant, and then turned back to Alan. "What did you expect? That's how Gordon is. You shared a room with him for years when you were boys."

"Yeah, but it's been awhile. I guess I forgot."

"Well, if it makes you feel any better, he put a sound chip in my electric shaver which played 'The Stars and Stripes Forever' at high volume."

"What did you do?"

"I snuck into his room and put the chip into his electric toothbrush. Virgil was just finishing putting the sprinkler into the ceiling. He said he spotted it in his own room before it could rain on him."

"Did Gordon get everybody?"

"I haven't heard from everybody, yet. Brains said Gordon had attempted to put singing mermaid pop-ups on his laptop computer, so he copied them to Gordon's. Instead of singing, Brains said the mermaids now wave a forefinger at the user and say 'no hacking.' I guess he's not going to touch Dad, though, and Dad told Gordon long ago that Kyrano's off limits."

Alan nodded.

"Go eat something; you'll feel better," Scott said. "I'll see if I can find where he put the chip in the plant."

After breakfast, Jeff again called the boys to an assembly session in the cargo hold--all except Scott, who was on bridge watch. Gordon arrived last of all. Although he stepped inside the hold gingerly, Jeff could hear "ouch, ouch, ouch" every time Gordon took a step. When Gordon drew even with John, John silently extended an arm, grinning and holding Gordon's shoes in his hand. Jeff then saw that Gordon was wearing John's running shoes. Looking sheepish, Gordon changed shoes and handed John's back to him. John placidly accepted the return of his running shoes, and placed them against the wall—John already was wearing his uniform shoes.

Jeff pointed to Gordon. "You have toothpaste on your earlobe."

"Oh." Gordon took a kerchief from his pocket and wiped his ear.

"Is it raining outside?" Jeff asked, noticing that Gordon's uniform shoulders were damp.

"Uh, no," Gordon said. "Malfunction with the sprinkler in my room."

"The same kind of malfunction that caused a sound chip to get into the heels of John's running shoes?" Jeff asked. When answered by silence, Jeff continued, "Nothing wrong with a little fun, boys, but let's not allow it to interfere with our duties, shall we?"

"Yeah, Dad."

"Sure, Dad."

"Okay, Dad."

"Whatever you say, Dad."

Jeff turned to Brains. "We'll start work on the power plant today."

In five days, the barge arrived at Tracy Island. They all gathered in the bridge to look it over as Gordon slowly circled their new home. The island was not very large; the rocks were gray and red and mostly barren. One side presented a rugged cliff face; the other showed a ledge in the midst of a slope descending to the sea.

"We're going to build the house on that ledge," Jeff said, pointing. "It will be able to withstand a category 6 hurricane."

"Don't they call them typhoons in this region?" Virgil said.

Jeff chuckled. "Right, Virgil."

"Our soundings showed natural caves w-w-within the rocks," Brains said. "We'll use those for hangars and storage."

Jeff turned around and looked at his sons. "I want to make it clear that this is our home now, and we're going to treat it as such."

"Well, sure, Dad," Alan said.

"That means that we're going to keep things clean and neat. There will be no littering, no half-eaten candy bars on the grounds, and most of all, if you need to go to the bathroom, you're going to use the bathrooms on the barge."

The younger men looked abashed; Scott answered for them all. "We got the message, Dad."

"Let's start unloading, then. Gordon, you can dock right about there."

Jeff, Virgil, and John had shown the others how to use the heavy construction equipment; many were industrial robots that could be controlled manually or programmed for a certain task. The robots resembled gigantic red cones, two to three stories high, with a narrow base, sprouting mechanical arms—some with two arms, some with four. Each had an indentation near the base with a control panel and seat for the operator. Along with Brains, they had put together a detailed step-by-step plan to build the hangars, the house—which Jeff had named Tracy Villa—the supporting infrastructures, and all the rescue equipment, including the aircraft.

First, however, they had to make an opening in a rock face in order to get into the caves inside. On previous visits to the island, Brains's soundings had revealed natural fissures in the stone. Now, Jeff, Virgil, and John, who had already done similar work on the moon, used the robots to carefully drill into those fissures and widen them, until a square piece of rock came loose. The robots then moved the piece—a mass easily weighing dozens of tons—safely to one side.

"Why not just use explosives and blast an opening?" Alan asked.

Countdown to Action! 73

Jeff and Brains turned to him. "Because that square piece of rock is going to be a hangar door," Jeff said.

Alan's brow furrowed, but he said nothing.

Jeff took a deep breath and released it. "We've done a good afternoon's work, boys. Let's have dinner and start again in the morning."

After dinner, Jeff set up a couple of deck chairs outside. Kyrano brought a tray with a couple of Mai Tais, handed Jeff one, and then took the other and sat next to him. They watched as Virgil set up his electronic keyboard and began to play a Joplin rag. John anchored his Dobsonian to the deck and began to align it for observing.

"Can you find the Tracy Nebula?" Alan asked him.

"No, you need a space telescope to see that," John said.

"What can you see?"

"At this time, you can get a good view of Jupiter and its moons."

"You can see the moons?"

"Take a look," John said.

Alan did. From his vantage point, Jeff marveled that the telescope stayed stable on the barge. On the other hand, the giant vessel did not rock much, particularly at anchor near the shore.

"Help! Help!" It was Gordon's voice.

Jeff and Kyrano were halfway out of their chairs when they saw Gordon running in their direction, firing an oversized water pistol over his shoulder at Scott, who sprinted behind him, firing back. The two older men sat again. When Gordon and Scott reached their other brothers, who had turned to watch the water duel, Gordon tossed extra squirt guns—tucked in his waistband—in their direction. Soon, all five of them joined in the horseplay, ducking and weaving, laughing and shouting. Gordon rolled on the deck, crossing his arms in front of him to fire at two brothers at once.

"I do not usually see Scott chasing his brothers," Kyrano remarked.

"Gordon started it." Jeff, with his hand around his drinking glass, gestured at his fourth son. "The extra water pistols show that he was spoiling for a fight. He probably squirted Scott, Scott grabbed another pistol, fired back, and chased him."

"I see." Kyrano took a sip of his drink. "They are fine boys, Jeff Tracy."

"Yes, they are."

"You have been a good father to them."

"Thank you."

"Nonetheless, I am glad I have a daughter."

Jeff chuckled. "I know what you mean."

The next day when Alan got up, he looked out the window of his cabin to see that they were in the midst of a tropical downpour. He was relieved that the room had two doors: one to the deck and the other to an interior passageway. He went down to the mess hall for breakfast and saw Virgil and John already there.

"Where's Dad?" Alan asked as he sat and reached for a plate of croissants.

"He and Scott and Gordon went out to check on things," Virgil said.

"In this weather?" Alan said.

"I guess when we start going on rescues, we'll work in all kinds of weather, just as we did when we were volunteer firefighters," John said. He put down his napkin and stood. "I'll go see if they need a hand."

"I guess I'll go down to the main hold and do some welding," Virgil said.

"I suppose I can hand you the parts," Alan said.

Virgil grinned.

"Just what do you think you're doing?" Jeff stood in the doorway of the hold, hands on hips, water dripping off his slicker.

Alan and Virgil turned toward him. "We're doing some welding, Father," Virgil said.

"That's not on the schedule for today. Now get on some rain gear and get out there."

"But it's raining buckets!" Alan said.

"You didn't seem to mind getting wet yesterday evening."

Alan extended an arm. "It's a torrent out there!"

"Once we're in operation, who do you think people are going to call if they need help in the middle of a hurricane?" Jeff demanded.

Virgil shut off the welding equipment and began to secure it. "I see what you mean."

"But we can't build anything in the rain," Alan said, "it won't hold together."

"What do you think it'll do, melt? Everything we have is designed to hold up in any kind of extreme, whether it's the moon or Antarctica. Now get going!"

Virgil, Alan observed, did not seem bothered by Jeff's reprimand. Once outside, he hummed as he worked and spoke with his father and brothers as if nothing had happened. Alan found he had no desire to engage in any kind of conversation—the rain was noisy anyway and they had to speak loudly to be heard—he simply set out the boundary markers for the runway as instructed.

Around noon, Jeff walked over. Alan had been glancing at his waterproof watch, hoping that they could at least go inside for lunch, but not daring to ask about it. "You all right, son?" Jeff asked. "You're not feeling ill, are you?"

Alan kept his eyes on his task. "No, Father."

"You know, you don't have to do this if you don't want to."

Alan knew his father was referring to belonging to the rescue organization; not simply setting out the markers in the rain. "No, it's all right."

"You sure?"

"Yes, Father." He wiped the rain off his face with the arm of his jacket; instantly, his face became wet again.

"Nothing will be said if you back out."

"I'm doing my job, aren't I?"

"Yes, you are. You've done a fine job all morning. I'm proud of you; it takes maturity to see a mistake and correct it. I hope you'll stay. But what I said before still stands. If your heart's not in this, you can walk away."

"I'm right here, Father."

Jeff put a hand on his shoulder. "So you are. Are you hungry? Let's go and have lunch." He waved at his other sons to join them.

* * *

That evening, Jeff walked into the empty mess hall. He smelled freshly-baked apple pie and freshly-ground coffee brewing. Through the wide serving window, he could see Kyrano in the kitchen, but the chef's attention was on a computer screen.

Jeff stepped to the window. "That pie sure smells good, Kyrano."

Kyrano turned. "It is almost done, Jeff Tracy."

Jeff smiled. "I can't wait. By the way, Scott and I got out the roto-tiller. The rain has stopped, and you can start working on your planting tomorrow."

"Thank you."

Jeff indicated the computer screen. "Anything interesting on the Internet news?"

"My half-brother was arrested by the Canadian authorities."

"Well, I'd say they got their man."

"They did, Jeff Tracy, but my brother has always said that no prison can hold him."

"Even if it can't, he's a long way from here. He can't know where you are, anyway."

"He has always seemed to find me, wherever I am."

Jeff raised his eyebrows. "I didn't know you had contact with him since you left Malaysia...not that it's any of my business," he hastened to add.

"I have not seen him often, and then only briefly," Kyrano said. "It will be years since I have seen him, and when I begin to think that I will see him no more, there he is."

"Does he ask you for anything?"

Kyrano shook his head. "He only says he is happy to see that I am well, and it seems to him that I am doing well, and he is on his way."

"Does Tin-Tin know?"

"She does not."

"Well, it's certain that he's not going to bother you here!"

"I would think not, and yet I am uneasy."

Jeff walked through the kitchen door and put a hand on Kyrano's shoulder. "There's nothing to fear, my friend. The boys and I will make sure no harm comes to you or Tin-Tin."

6

Once Bela Ghat walked through the doors of the prison's atrium, the guard removed the handcuffs. The prison, just outside Vancouver, was a modern one. A huge skylight, six stories above, let in ample sunlight. Green plants lined the walls. The red carpeting showed no dirt or wear. It might be mistaken for a hotel, if it were not for the guard station, one story up, from which the atrium and all cells were in clear view. The guard escorted Ghat to a cell and motioned inside. "Your new home, Ghat," he said, and walked away.

Inside the cell, Ghat saw a pale, wizened man sitting on a cot, reading a book. The man's arms and face were speckled with brown spots, which extended even to his scalp. Ghat could see the spotting through the thin, white hair—what there was of it.

Ghat approached the cot. "Hello, Uncle Bob," he said softly.

Bob glanced up at him. "Hmph." His gaze returned to his book. "And how did you get here?"

"Pulled over, as usual. The officer looked me up and found the international warrants out on me."

"I'd think you could get out of that!"

"Oh, then I wouldn't have been able to see you again!"

Bob looked up at him. "So that's it. Need something from your old Uncle Bob."

Ghat twisted around to peer at the guard station. They could see him and his uncle, yes, but they could not hear, not at this distance. He took a minute to casually inspect the surroundings; no obvious listening devices, either. Further, he had done his homework, getting the plans and budget for the prison weeks ago through his contacts. No communication systems except for the devices the guards wore to talk to each other, and no payments for electronic eavesdropping devices in the prison cells or budgeted salaries for personnel to listen to them. He felt confident that he could have a private conversation.

He sat on the cot next to his uncle. "I need more information from you."

Bob snorted. "What could that be? I taught you all you know."

"But I do not have the ability to read minds. Or control them."

Bob raised his book and turned his attention to it. "You've done just fine from all I've heard."

"Oh, yes, I can persuade people. But I cannot command them." When Bob appeared to be engrossed in his reading again, Ghat added urgently, in a low voice, "You said the ancient rites would give me great powers of the mind!"

Tossing the book on the bed, Bob turned to his nephew. "And how many other people do you know who can do what you can?"

"All that happens when I concentrate is that my victim falls into a deep sleep," Ghat complained.

Bob waved his hand. "And how many men here wouldn't give 10 years of their life to have that power?"

"But I want more!"

Ghat's uncle got up, strode to a shelf, and picked up a small box. He took a small white stick and put it in his mouth as if it were a toothpick. "Damned jail. Can't smoke. Can't get tobacco hardly anywhere nowadays. Have to settle for nicotine candy, and even that's hard to trade for."

"Why don't you get out?"

The old man turned to him. "When you get to be my age, the mind doesn't work the way it did." He sucked at the stick. "Besides, Hank Stone told me that if I ever got out, he'd use me as shark bait."

Ghat sighed. "Then there is nothing more?"

Bob sat back on the cot. "The ancient magicians were just as frustrated as you. Look, these things don't always work the way people want." Bob shook his head. "It certainly didn't for me."

Ghat hung his head.

"There is one thing," Bob said, and Ghat snapped to attention. "How I kept track of you, dear nephew."

"What's that?"

"When there is a blood tie, a magician may," he held up a finger, "and I say 'may,' learn some thoughts if a person is ready to speak them, perhaps even plant suggestions. You need part of a person—in these modern times, we say DNA—and fashion an image bearing it, using it as a focus."

"And you used this on me?" Ghat said, astonished.

He shrugged. "My dear sister, your mother, wanted me to keep an eye on you. Remember when you came to visit, shortly after I moved to Canada?"

Ghat twitched his thick black eyebrows, thinking. "I was...10 years old?"

"Nine. I took a hair, from your pillow—" he looked over at his nephew—"you had hair then, and pushed it into the wax I used to make an image of you. It is easier to make images nowadays, with computers and lasers. People can even buy a kit in a store to do it."

"I thought you made that because you loved me."

The old man patted his arm. "And so I do, dear nephew. But I needed to keep you out of trouble until you were old enough and smart enough to escape the clutches of the law yourself."

Ghat frowned. "That means the only one I could control would be my worthless half-brother, Kyrano."

"Worthless? Your father's estate wasn't worthless! Barbara would never have married him if it was!"

"But I already had that...and sold it, and built my own estate far beyond the reach of the law."

Bob rubbed his hands contemplatively. "Well, I hear that he is a friend of Jeff Tracy. He's worth a fortune, or so I understand."

Ghat's face brightened. "Yes...yes, he must know a way to get to him."

"And, as I've always said, it's just as easy to cheat a rich man as a poor one...sometimes easier."

For the first time in the conversation, Ghat smiled. "Thank you, Uncle."

The next morning, Ghat awakened to see three people surrounding his uncle's cot: two guards and a nurse.

The nurse shook his head. "Must have died in his sleep."

The shorter guard used his communications device to call for a stretcher.

The taller guard turned to Ghat. "You notice anything?"

Ghat shook his head, then motioned to the guard station. "You can see everything. You would know better than I."

"Well, he was an old man," the nurse observed.

"Since you just got here yesterday, I suppose you didn't know him well," the taller guard said to Ghat.

"I barely knew him at all," Ghat said innocently.

By the time of the water show, the Tracys and Brains had built the runway, bordered by a gravel area which extended 50 feet to either side. The artificial palm trees had been set next to the concrete, on pivots so that the trees could be tilted to the side, to allow for the wingspan for the yet-to-be-built heavy rescue airship.

"Very nice," Scott said, standing next to Jeff on the gravel skirt. They looked up to the control room built into the top of the cliff, which they called "Cliff House." From there, through the hurricane-proof windows, they could see Gordon, sitting in the control room, amusing himself by pressing the radio controls so the palm trees tilted away, then up, then away, then up again.

"No one will suspect we have a giant aircraft with the palm trees so close to the edge of the runway," Jeff remarked.

Next, Gordon tested the hydraulic lift. This brought a section of the runway up to a 45 degree angle and would help launch the airship. At the base, a smaller section tilted up so that most of the exhaust would be vented underground into empty volcanic chambers.

"You're sure that the missile defense satellites won't pick that up?" Scott asked. "When I took my turn at the World Defense Command, I could pick up test firings of short- and medium-range rockets, as well as ICBMs."

"It was the same when I was in the Air Force," Jeff said. "But Brains designed the engines so that the exhaust will fit the profile of a twin engine jet aircraft, not a missile. With the other two craft, which would resemble a missile firing, ignition will occur underground."

The hydraulic lift went flat again, but this time metal poles sprouted from the ground, with curved tops resembling a gooseneck lamp.

Countdown to Action! 81

"As soon as we hook those up to the tanks with the foam, our fire suppression system will be in place," Jeff observed.

The poles disappeared, and Scott turned to the pier at the end of the runway. Gordon tilted it down into the ocean, using the controls.

"Visitors will think it's a boat dock or runway extension," Jeff said. "But that will be the emergency launch for the submarine."

"I'm sure Gordon loves it," Scott said, as the pier went up again.

Finally, the rock face on the cliff below the Cliff House went down, showing an enormous rock cavern behind. As the stone hangar door disappeared, and the metal bridge that spanned the narrow rectangular hole holding the slab lowered into place, one of the artificial shrubs got caught and crushed.

"Uh oh," Scott said. "We'll have to move that."

"Watch," Jeff said.

Sure enough, when Gordon raised the hangar door again, the shrub unfolded, good as new.

"Well, I'll be," Scott said.

Jeff waved at Gordon and spoke into his personal transmitter, set into his wristwatch. "Okay, son, everything so far works according to plan. Let's get ready to go to the water show. You all deserve a break after working so hard for the past month."

Gordon let out a triumphant yell, which Scott could hear even through his father's receiver.

Brains elected to stay behind and watch everything, not that they expected any visitors. The rest of the Tracys, and Kyrano, boarded the helijet, which Jeff and Scott piloted to Honolulu. Once there, they rented a van. Alan drove to the beach, and the Tracys got out. Kyrano slid into the driver's seat to go to the open market to buy fresh food.

While his brothers and father stood by, Gordon checked in to the water show's headquarters and got his power boat assignment.

"Hey, Gordon!" called a tanned, blond-haired man walking toward him. He waved.

"Sam Burnside! I haven't seen you since the Miami show!" Gordon called back. "Say, could you do me a favor?"

"Sure!"

"They gave me the blue boat. I always take the yellow one. The yellow one's yours, would you trade?"

Sam shrugged. "The officials say they're giving us all the same model, Gordon, so it doesn't matter to me. Go ahead and take the yellow one."

"Thanks!"

Sam punched Gordon playfully on the side of the arm. "I thought this was going to be an easy win, until you showed up!"

Gordon grinned back at him. "I'll be sure not to get too far ahead of you."

Sam chuckled. "Not too far behind me, you mean!" He leaned to one side, and waved. "See you got your Dad and brothers with you. Hi, Mr. Tracy! Scott, Virgil, John, Alan!"

They all waved back. "Hi, Sam!" they called.

Sam climbed into the blue power boat while Gordon walked to the yellow machine. Along with the water show's mechanics, he carefully inspected the vehicle, then put on his racing suit. Just before he put his helmet on, Jeff, who had been watching closely, said, "Signed off on the safety checklist?"

Gordon smiled, "Yes, Dad, everything's fine. I'd have a greater chance of getting injured crossing the street."

Even so, Jeff could not take his eyes away until the mechanics strapped Gordon in his pilot's seat, and lowered the top. Glancing at the shore, he saw an ambulance, with paramedics standing by—required by law at such events.

"Don't worry, Dad," Alan said as they walked off the dock. "Modern power boats have just as many safety features and backups as modern racing cars."

"And Gordon has a good head on his shoulders," John added.

The water show officials directed them to a viewing stand where the Tracys found they had been assigned excellent seats. They could see everything clearly, from the opening ceremonies to the water ski displays. The power boat race, at the climax, brought them to their feet, cheering, as Gordon wove in and out and around the competitors. Gordon and Sam alternated in taking the lead several times, until, just at the finish line, Gordon

Countdown to Action! 83

pulled ahead by a nose. The program then called for precision routines, where Gordon and the other boats maneuvered in various formations, from the simple to the complicated. Gordon even "skipped" over the water, causing his craft to "jump" over other boats. Once, he even flipped the power boat 360 degrees to land again smoothly on the water's surface. The crowd cheered and applauded.

Virgil leaned over to Jeff. "You know, Dad, Sam's engine is running too hard."

"Yeah," Scott said, "I hear it, too...as if he's holding the throttle open."

"...or the throttle is stuck open," John added.

"We'd better report it to the officials," Jeff said, rising from his seat. "It could be a safety hazard."

"I've seen it in automobiles...sudden acceleration...you can't stop the car no matter how hard you hit the brakes," Alan added, following Jeff and his other brothers.

The racing officials immediately radioed Sam to come in. They could see Sam break formation and guide the boat to the dock. Fortunately, it seemed to be slowing. Mechanics surrounded the machine, and lifted up the top hatch. Sam motioned to the mechanics as the engine continued to rumble softly; one of the mechanics popped the engine hood and grabbed a cutting tool, apparently ready to snip the ignition wires to get it to stop.

"Well, that's one accident avoided," Alan said from the shore.

Meanwhile, Gordon and the other boats, finished with their routines, flocked back to the pier. The rest of the Tracys walked to where the show staff members were securing Gordon's boat. Gordon opened the hatch, climbed out, and stood on the bow, perfectly balanced as the vessel rocked gently back and forth with the waves.

"Watch out!"

At the same time Jeff heard Sam's frantic shout and the roar of a revived engine out of control, he saw Sam's boat glance off the other boats, run up and over the boat behind Gordon—that pilot had already left the boat—and hit Gordon on the back. Gordon flew up and into the water, away from the pier. Sam's boat landed on the beach as panicked spectators ran in all directions, creating an empty space. The engine's jets spurted out sand and water, then ground to a halt.

Meanwhile, Scott tore off his sunglasses, kicked off his sandals, and dove in after Gordon. The other Tracy brothers moved to follow, but Jeff shouted, "Wait!" He called to Alan, "Get Dr. West on the phone! Tell him to meet us at the Honolulu Trauma Center! John, Virgil, get a backboard from the ambulance!" He tossed his own sunglasses aside, jerked his shoes off, and dove after Scott.

Gordon still had his helmet and racing suit on. The power boat racing suits had been designed to inflate at the touch of water. As a result, Gordon's head remained above water and the rest of his body was held immobile by the suit. Scott already had a grip on the suit's shoulder, and was swimming to shore with his brother in hand. Jeff reached them moments later and held Gordon's other shoulder.

"He's breathing," Scott called over to Jeff.

Gordon moaned.

"You'll be okay, Gordon," Jeff said in a loud voice. "Just hold on!"

John and Virgil splashed out from the beach with the backboard, and the four of them, experienced by their own paramedic training, secured Gordon to the board without bending him. The paramedics met them as they emerged from the water.

"We'll take it from here," one of them said.

Alan called, "Dad, Dr. West is already here! He came to see the show!"

Sure enough, the tall blond doctor stood beside Alan, and stepped forward as the paramedics headed to the ambulance. "I want him on a pain cocktail, stat!" His native Texas accent still showed in his speech, even after years of residence in Hawaii.

Jeff paused and turned to his sons. "I'll ride in the ambulance. You get a taxi and meet us at the hospital. Stop and buy a new laptop with a webcam on the way." He hurried to the ambulance and got in. One of the paramedics climbed into the driver's seat as the other shut the door. West had already cut Gordon's suit open at the arm and was applying an IV. Jeff heard the siren sound and felt the ambulance accelerate.

"Dad," Gordon croaked painfully.

Jeff leaned over him. "Easy, son. Best not to talk right now."

"Don't stop."

Jeff took Gordon's limp hand in his. "I won't."

"Stop what, Jeff?" West asked curiously.

"Uh...we're building a house on our south sea island retreat."

West smiled and addressed Gordon. "Then you have something to look forward to, Gordon. I'll see that you get there." West and Jeff both looked at the autonurse, already taking note of Gordon's vital signs. He was stable...for the moment.

Back at the beach, Sam, helmet under his arm, ran up to the remaining four Tracy brothers. "Oh my gosh! Oh my gosh! I'm so sorry! I couldn't stop it! I tried, but...."

He was interrupted my Alan's fist hitting his face.

Scott grabbed Alan's arm and spun him around. "Walk away!" he ordered.

Alan turned back. "But...!"

Scott spun Alan around again. "I said 'walk away!'"

Sam held his face and sobbed. "I'm sorry. I'm so sorry."

John put a hand on Sam's shoulder. "We know it was an accident. Are you okay?"

Sam worked his jaw tentatively. "I think so."

"Okay," Virgil said, holding the sunglasses and shoes that he had gathered from the dock. "Put an ice pack on your face."

"Is Gordon going to be okay?"

"Hand me your cell phone," John said, and Sam handed it over. John got out his own cell phone and made some adjustments to both. "We'll text you when we know anything." He gave Sam's phone back and put his own away.

Sam held his face, inclined his head slightly, and left.

Scott turned to Alan. "What's wrong with you, boy?"

"He's ruined everything!"

"It was an accident," Scott insisted. "You of all people know it's impossible to stop an engine when the throttle's stuck open."

Alan shook his head.

Virgil patted Alan's back. "We'll manage to get the job done without Gordon."

"Oh, do you know how to build a submarine?"

"No, but we can build everything else, and when Gordon gets back, we can help him with the rest."

"If he gets back," Alan said.

"We don't know that he won't, yet," John said. "He may not be hurt as bad as it seems."

"Seems bad enough," Alan said.

"Well we won't find out standing here," Scott said. "Let's get the taxi and meet Dad at the trauma center. There's an electronics store just down the street." He turned to John. "John, call Kyrano and tell him what's happened."

Once Ghat had escaped from the Vancouver prison—a simple task, for him—he made his way to Honolulu. From there, he had hoped to find some leads that would tell him which Pacific island Jeff Tracy had settled on. Shortly after his arrival, however, he began to see advertisements for an upcoming water show, featuring Gordon Tracy. Where the son was, could the father be far behind? And his half-brother would probably be with them....

Ghat needed something from Kyrano—a hair would probably be the easiest thing to get. He carried a small pair of scissors and a small envelope in his pocket for the purpose. Once he made an image and put in the hair, Kyrano would be in his power, no matter what the distance. But first, he had to get the hair. Ghat had no doubt that if an image of Kyrano with a hair of Kyrano embedded into it would connect him with Kyrano's mind, then being in direct contact with Kyrano himself, holding onto the skin of the arms with his hands, would give him an even greater power.

On the day of the water show, Ghat prowled the open-air food markets. He had already visited the water show dock early in the morning and made a little adjustment to Gordon Tracy's boat to insure that the Tracys would stay busy. Sure enough, it was not very long before he spotted his brother at a distance, loading crates of fresh fruits and vegetables into a van with a rental sticker. Scanning the area, Ghat saw few people near the van, and none behind the van. Capitalizing on the opportunity, Ghat padded into the alley where the van was parked, circling

Countdown to Action!

to approach Kyrano from behind. When Kyrano turned to pick up the next crate, he stood face-to-face with Ghat. He gasped as Ghat seized him.

"Kyrano...you are in my power," Ghat said in a low voice. "It is useless to resist me." He gazed right into Kyrano's eyes. "Now...tell me where Jeff Tracy's island is."

"No...no," Kyrano moaned softly.

Images flooded into Ghat's mind, but not the ones he expected. Instead of an island, he saw sophisticated flying machines, and heard a name in his head: International Rescue. This was even better! His customers in the arms trade would pay millions--no, billions!—for such aircraft.

"More, I need to see more," Ghat insisted.

"No...,"

"Sir? Sir, you forgot the meat locker!" the grocer called.

Immediately, Ghat released Kyrano. Kyrano slipped to the ground. Ghat whipped out the scissors and snipped a lock of hair. Then he ran. From a safe distance, Ghat turned and saw the grocer standing over Kyrano.

"Are you okay?"

Slowly, Kyrano sat and touched his head. "Yes...it seems I had a dizzy spell."

"Should I call 911?"

"No...I am fine."

"I heard voices; were you talking to someone?"

"No, I was here alone. Perhaps you heard someone walking by with a cell phone."

"Speaking of which, yours is ringing."

Ghat smiled as he saw Kyrano take out his cell phone, and strolled away triumphantly. His half-brother had no memory of the mind probe. Excellent! Then Kyrano would not alert the authorities of his presence. Even better, Ghat now knew of the Tracys' secret project. And secret it would stay, because he would not have any other arms dealer attempt to get to those machines before he did. Further, with the Tracy machines known only to him, he could take his time. There was no hurry. He could make his way back to his retreat, fashion the image of Kyrano, and check in now and again to monitor their progress. Then, when they went into operation, he would strike!

7

Jeff and Scott sat in the waiting room of the trauma center, adjusting the newly-purchased laptop. Virgil and John occupied themselves with a video game on John's cell phone. Alan paced. When Kyrano came in, Jeff gave the laptop to Scott and stood.

"How is Gordon?" Kyrano asked.

"We're waiting for the MRI results," Jeff said. Spotting West walking toward them, he added, "That must be it."

The other Tracys stood and surrounded West.

"The good news," the doctor said, "is that the spinal cord is intact. He's not paralyzed. He's lucky to still have had that helmet on and the protective suit. And there's no permanent head or brain injury, though there is a severe whiplash."

Virgil breathed a loud sigh of relief and clapped a smiling John on the shoulder.

"What's the bad news?" Jeff asked.

"He has fractures of the vertebrae. Plus four rib fractures," he put his hand on his side to indicate, "and a lot of soft tissue damage. He's going to be here a while."

"I want the latest technology used. Whatever it takes, whatever it costs," Jeff insisted.

West nodded. "He's still going to be here a while. Even with state-of-the-art techniques, healing takes time."

"Can we see him?"

"We lowered his body temperature to keep the swelling down, and induced a coma, so he won't be able to talk to you."

"I still want to see him. And I want a private duty nurse with him 24 hours a day."

West nodded. "I thought you would. I already arranged for that."

"Thanks." Jeff gestured to a tall, sturdy woman in a Tracy Technologies security uniform. "I also want a security guard standing outside the door. I don't want the tabloid press taking pictures of the former Olympic gold medalist in a hospital bed. We've already had your hospital security turn photographers away."

West sighed. "Yes, I remember the reporters swarming around when Alan broke a rib after the crash in his first Grand Prix. I'll coordinate with hospital security."

Alan rolled his eyes when his name was mentioned, but said nothing.

"Meanwhile, y'all can see Gordon for a few moments." West gestured for them to follow. They quietly entered the intensive care unit, where they saw Gordon in a bed, with the autonurse equipment monitoring his vitals, and an IV in his arm. A male nurse sat nearby. Scott set the laptop on a nearby table and adjusted it.

Jeff leaned over the bed and put a hand on Gordon's shoulder. "Gordon, this is Dad. You're going to be fine. We're leaving a laptop here so we can see you anytime we want. Once you're able, you can call us and talk to us." He kissed Gordon's forehead. "We'll be back to see you again." He straightened and turned to the male nurse. "That laptop stays right where it is, within a clear view of Gordon. If he wants to use it, let him use it."

The nurse nodded.

Jeff turned to his other sons. "Okay, boys, say good-bye to your brother."

"We aren't going to just leave him here!" Alan said.

West put a hand on Alan's arm. "There's nothing you can do here. You'd just be in the way. He's going to sleep most of the day for the next few days."

"You'll start therapy once he is awake?" Jeff asked.

"Oh, yes," West said. "My patients always complain I get them out of bed before they're ready."

"Good," Jeff said.

Meanwhile, Scott, Virgil, John, and finally, Alan, bent over Gordon to say farewell. Kyrano added that he would bring Gordon some food when he was ready for it. Jeff spoke a few words to the security guard, who had taken a position outside Gordon's door, and they left the hospital.

When they reached the van, Jeff noticed Alan's sullen expression. "I'll drive."

"Fine," Alan said listlessly, and tossed him the keys.

On the ride back to the airport, Alan sat in the front passenger's seat, slumped as much as the shoulder harness would allow, hands in his pockets.

Scott leaned forward and spoke to Jeff. "I don't think Gordon's ever been seriously ill since he was a baby."

Alan straightened a little and turned to Scott. "I hadn't heard about that."

Scott explained, though the events were riveted in Jeff's brain. Gordon had weighed in at just over 5 pounds at birth, even though he was full term. Jeff's Dad called Gordon "the runt of the litter," which caused Lucy to chuckle and Jeff to frown. Runt, hell! No son of his was a "runt!"

Once the doctor certified Lucy and Gordon as healthy, they came home to a very excited set of brothers. Two-year-old John immediately became their baby monitor ("Mommy, baby cry!" "Mommy, baby 'wake." "Mommy, baby sleepy!"), while Scott and Virgil would gently rock the baby to sleep when they set his carrier on the floor. The first night, as they put him to bed, however, Gordon did not look right to them. Lucy immediately called the doctor and held Gordon up to the telephone's viewscreen. The doctor said Gordon probably had a mild case of jaundice and told her to bring him to the hospital.

Lucy wrapped Gordon in blankets and put him in the carrier. As long as they were going out, she gave Jeff both the infant seat and the handle of a bag of trash to put in the can in the garage.

John started crying hysterically, clutching at Jeff's trousers. Once Lucy calmed him down, they discovered that their lecture to John the week before about what trash was and where it went led him to believe that they were "throwing baby 'way." Jeff said, gently but firmly, "No, John, Gordon is a member of our family and we do not throw family away."

Just as Jeff thought the matter was settled, Virgil, unexpectedly, let out a wail. It turned out that he remembered that the original baby carrier, purchased just the month before, had to be returned because it was defective. "No, Virgil," Jeff assured him, "Gordon is not defective and we're not giving him back. He's ours now, and we're taking him to the hospital because he doesn't feel well and they will make him better."

"Daddy...," Scott said tentatively.

Jeff sighed. "What is it, son?" he asked, as calmly as he could.

"Gordon's not going to die, is he?"

Lucy crouched so she could look Scott in the eye. "No, Scott," she said, putting a hand on Scott's arm. "He's just a little sick, and Daddy and I should be back with him before breakfast. You watch your brothers, and mind Grandpa and Grandma now."

Once at the hospital, the doctor examined Gordon and had him placed under some lamps. He and Lucy watched Gordon sucking placidly on his pacifier as he napped under the lights... the only person not traumatized by the experience, it seemed. The nurses marveled at him, saying that a lot of babies cried while under the lights. While they were there, Lucy's cell phone rang with congratulations from her lady friends, and Jeff's rang with congratulations from his fellow astronauts—although Jeff spent a significant amount of time away from home at the moon base, he always made sure he took a generous amount of parental leave when each son was born. The parents among the astronauts assured Jeff that jaundice in newborns was not that unusual—though Jeff had never heard of it before—and generally not that serious. When he compared notes with Lucy, he found her friends had said the same.

Scott and Virgil were still up when Jeff and Lucy brought Gordon home, though he would still require three more light treatments. Upon explaining what happened to Gordon, Virgil insisted on shining his flashlight on his baby brother, and Lucy held him up to the crib to make it easier.

From the hallway door, Scott looked up at Jeff. "Will that really help Gordon?"

"It will help Virgil, and when someone wants to help, that's always good. And, Gordon will know that he has a brother who loves him."

"Should I shine my flashlight on him, too?"

Jeff smiled. "Gordon knows you love him, son; just as Virgil and John do...because you always help them."

"Okay, Daddy."

Lucy took Scott and Virgil to bed. Jeff went to the crib and lifted the ginger-haired Gordon gently, cradling him in his arms. Gordon slept on. Although Jeff knew that the idea that his infant son would absorb the strength in his arms was as irrational as Virgil's shining his flashlight on his baby brother, it nonetheless made him feel he was doing something to help Gordon, too. "You'll get better, son," he said softly. "I'll make sure you will."

Once Scott had told Alan the story, the van became quiet, and the silence extended to the helijet ride back to Tracy Island. John took the initiative to tell Brains what had happened to Gordon as the others helped Kyrano unload the groceries. Kyrano had purchased fresh fish from the market, packed in ice for the journey home. He set up a grill on the beach to cook them, and added fresh pineapple and vegetables. The others took plates and utensils from the portable table when dinner was ready. Once served, they sat on blankets on the beach to eat their meals.

Scott indicated the laptop on the ground next to Jeff with his fork. "Is that tuned to Gordon?"

"Yup," Jeff said, and slid it aside so Scott could see his brother on the screen. Gordon looked the same as he had when they left, hours before.

"Now we're a man short," Alan said, keeping his eyes on his food.

"Yes, we're a man short," Jeff affirmed. "But we go on, just the same."

"It won't be the same without Gordon," Alan countered.

"No, it won't," Jeff said. "But Gordon will rejoin us eventually. We aren't on a deadline. We'll still accomplish what we came for, it'll just take a little longer."

Alan sighed. "I still think we should have stayed with Gordon," he murmured.

"Gordon didn't want that. He wanted us to keep going. He told me, himself."

"Just what would you have done?" Scott asked. "The only thing we could have done was to sit by his bedside. There's nothing we could do to make him better."

"He'd know we were there."

Scott pointed to the laptop. "We can talk to him whenever we want." He looked at the laptop. "Uh, the sound is off on that right now, isn't it? He can't hear what we're saying?"

Jeff nodded.

"I know how you feel, Alan," John said, "but really, if we had stayed in the hospital, we wouldn't have spent that much time with him, anyway. The nursing staff would have rushed us out for one thing or another, and we would've ended up just wandering around the city or swimming at the beach."

"We couldn't all fit comfortably in that room at the same time anyway," Virgil added. "It was crowded enough when we said good-bye. We would have had to take shifts. We might as well be here, in that case."

"We'll go back and see Gordon every Sunday," Jeff said. "And if he really needs us, we're just a few hours away by helijet."

"Gordon had s-s-signed off on the plans for the s-s-submarine before you left for Honolulu," Brains interjected. "All we need to do is follow the plan and build it."

"Well, any of us could do that!" Scott said confidently.

"Sure," Virgil said, looking around at his brothers. "Every one of us has been trained in engineering..."

"...space station repair, communications...," John added.

"...even scuba diving and piloting all sorts of aircraft," Scott said. "I reckon any of us could do just about anything."

Alan's brow furrowed. "Yes...," he said slowly. "I hadn't thought of that before, but we have." His gaze wandered to Jeff, who met his eye as Alan continued, "...almost as if it was planned."

Jeff's expression did not change. He stared solemnly at his youngest son.

Alan pointed at Jeff. "You were training us, just for this." He pointed at the ground. "Your very own rescue team. That's why we all served in the civil air patrol, the volunteer fire department... you were getting us all ready to serve you!" He shook his head. "And all of us fools just went right along with it. Lucky you."

Jeff maintained eye contact, but did not respond.

"Well, that's it. I'm done. I'm not going to be a chess piece on your board, to move wherever you want. I'm choosing my own destiny." He took up his plate and utensils and stomped back to the barge.

Jeff turned back to the plate of apple pie that Kyrano had served for dessert, and carved a bite-sized piece with his fork.

The young men looked from one to the other. Finally, Scott turned to Jeff. "I'm sure he'll cool off and change his mind, Dad."

Jeff shook his head. "He hasn't seemed very happy from day one on the barge. Go ahead and use the helijet; take him wherever he wants to go."

"You're not going to stop him?" Scott asked.

"Nope."

"We'll be another man short," John pointed out.

"Yup." Jeff chewed his apple pie thoughtfully.

John turned to Brains. "Can we still build everything with just the five of us?"

Brains nodded. "We could if it were only Mr. Tracy and me. J-j-just slower."

"I guess that's a relief," Virgil said. He looked over at Jeff. "What if Alan changes his mind later, Dad?"

"Then he can come back," Jeff said evenly. "But I told you boys from the beginning...this is a hard task we're doing, and I don't want you doing it unless you're willing to give it everything you've got."

"Did you have us just to make a team?" Virgil asked. "Not that I want to leave or anything, I'm just curious."

"Well, your mother and I talked about having a large family even before we married," Jeff said. "I told her that since she's the one that had to do the hardest work, being pregnant and nursing and all, it was up to her. Fortunately, your mother wasn't the type to get sick during pregnancy. And I was proud of each and every one of you, from the moment you were born."

"Were you training us?" John asked.

"Even if I'd never thought of International Rescue, I would have encouraged you go to join the Scouts or Civil Air Patrol or volunteer fire department. I think we all need to do what we can to make the world a better place."

"Well, I certainly would have joined all of those organizations even if you'd never suggested them, Father," Scott said.

"Me, too," Virgil said.

"So would I." John added, "What would you have done if we'd all said no, if you don't mind my asking?"

"I'd find someone else." He motioned to Brains. "Brains, here, for instance, was all for the idea. And, I've already enlisted some other people I can trust. There's this former intelligence agent in England, for instance, a Lady Penelope Creighton-Ward. She's volunteered to do any undercover work we need."

"Wow," John said. "You really thought this out."

Jeff took a toothpick and applied it to his teeth. "Had to."

Scott found Alan packing his things in his cabin. "So, you really are serious about leaving?"

"I don't like feeling manipulated. Don't you?"

"No, I don't feel manipulated at all. Neither do Virgil or John, and I know Gordon didn't."

"Well, I do." He zipped up his suitcase. "Will you fly me to Honolulu?"

"Sure. Are you planning to watch over Gordon?"

"I'll pay him a visit. I'm going to bring him that plant. That'll bring a smile to his face."

"Ficus? Oh yeah, I never did find the talking chip."

"Then I'll go join Kenny in Florida. He invited me to stay with him for a while."

"Then what?"

"Get back in to racing, I guess. Maybe try the national circuit."

Scott shifted his weight and scratched his forehead. "You know, even though your mind's made up, I really feel I need to point out that Dad financed your racing career without any hesitation whatsoever...from the race driver training school in England when you were sixteen to your Grand Prix pit crew."

"Yeah, well...."

"And I don't remember you objecting to scuba lessons, or the civil air patrol, or anything else...in fact, it was all Dad could do to keep you from trying those before you reached the minimum age."

Alan lifted his chin. "That just shows how good he is at manipulating us...we thought they were all our own ideas."

"They were," Scott said plainly. "Do you think it was Dad's idea for John to get his radio licenses, or for Gordon to enlist in the aquanaut corps?"

Alan looked Scott in the eye. "You guys can do whatever you want to do. I'm doing what I need to do."

"Okay," Scott said. "But I think you're making a big mistake."

"I don't."

"Well, just keep in mind that you can come back whenever you want. Dad said so."

"Don't count on it."

Six weeks later, with the help of the industrial robots, the hangars and supporting structures were all built. That included the round house over the space vehicle launch bay, and the pool, which had to be mounted on rails to slide over the rocket reconnaissance vehicle launch bay.

They all stood on the runway to admire their work. "It's beginning to take shape," John said.

"Yes, you've all done a great job," Jeff said. "But there's a lot left to do."

Scott turned to Brains. "What's next?"

Brains consulted his PDA. "The pods and pod vehicles."

"When do we build the house?" Virgil asked.

"After that." Brains said.

"And the main vehicles?" Scott asked.

"Last of all," Jeff said. "And we have to build the scaffolding for those before we even start."

Scott blew out a breath. "A long road ahead of us."

Jeff clapped Scott on the shoulder. "But there's an end, and we'll reach it. Let's go see Gordon."

When they got to Gordon's hospital room, they saw Gordon sitting up in bed. Dr. West was removing the back brace. He glanced over at Jeff and said, "Gordon's made remarkable progress. We're sending him to the rehab center today."

"Good," Jeff said.

West turned to Gordon. "Now there's the work of physical therapy, to get you walking and running again, and to regain the full use of your hands and feet."

Gordon reached and scratched behind a shoulder. "I can do pretty well right now."

West leaned back and folded his arms. "Yes, the nursing staff told me that you somehow programmed the heart monitor to play 'Yankee Doodle.'"

Gordon grinned.

"But your nursing assistant says that using your laptop is still awkward for you, and it takes a while for you to pull the peripherals in and out." West touched his thumb and forefinger together. "So we still need to work on those fine motor skills, in addition to the walking."

"Will I be able to play the piano?"

The doctor took a breath. "Well, that depends, Gordon. Were you able to play the piano before?"

Scott put a hand to Gordon's forehead. "You must still be sick to think he'd fall for that old joke."

"Aw, Scott...." Gordon pushed his hand away.

Scott looked around. "Speaking of jokes, what happened to Ficus?"

"Oh, I donated that to the children's wing. The kids loved it."

"That talking plant was quite a sensation around here," West added.

"I'll bet," Scott said.

"Can we go with him to the rehab center?" Jeff asked West.

"Sure. Just follow us out and then follow the medicab."

Gordon leaned forward eagerly. "Did you bring the food?"

Jeff chuckled. "Yes, Kyrano sent another week's supply of food. We'll take it to the rehab center and leave it there."

"I must say," West said, "everyone on staff here has been talking about Gordon's food. No one thought that packaged and preserved food would taste any good, but Gordon's been thriving on it, and we've even had to lock it away to keep the staff here from sneaking a taste."

Jeff nodded. "Kyrano's an expert at that. When he worked for NASA, he would send up a three-month supply of food at a time and the last of it was as fresh and tasty as the first."

"Where is Kyrano?" Gordon asked.

"He stayed behind so Brains could come this time," Virgil said. "We needed to pick up more electronic parts."

West turned to Jeff. "Speaking of food, before you leave you might want to check out the new restaurant that opened up around here. It's run by a Texan who has beef flown in fresh from a cattle ranch every day. If you'll hand me your PDA, I'll give you the GPS coordinates."

Jeff gave him the device. "Thanks."

Despite Gordon's protests that he did not need one, the hospital staff put him on a gurney to go into the medicab and on to the rehab center. Jeff wondered about that, too, until he saw the nursing assistant help transfer Gordon from gurney to bed and noticed that Gordon's movements were still stiff and awkward.

Gordon settled back into the bed with a sigh, unable to completely hide his exhaustion from the transfer.

Jeff bent over him and patted his arm. "Your main task, son, will be to rebuild your stamina. That's going to take a while, even if you can walk and maneuver."

Gordon nodded slightly.

"We'll be back next week," Jeff said in farewell. The others said their goodbyes and left the room. When they stopped at the administration desk to see that the records were in order, the rehab administrator said, "Now, don't you worry, Mr. Tracy. This is the best rehab center in the islands. We have weight training, low-impact sports and games, yoga, tai chi, jacuzzis, hot tubs, and an Olympic-sized pool."

The Tracys and Brains exchanged glances. Jeff finished signing the necessary forms and waved a farewell.

As they walked out, Scott leaned over to Jeff and said in a low voice, "Do you think we should tell them?"

Jeff shook his head slightly and murmured, "No."

They found the Texas Ranch Restaurant very easily, with its huge sign in the front, lettering set on an outline of the state of Texas. The server, a young woman, escorted them to a large booth. Jeff and Scott sat on one side, Virgil and John on the other, and Brains on a chair on the aisle.

As they looked over the menus, Virgil said to Scott, "Did you see the list of beers?"

Scott nodded. "Yeah."

Jeff looked up. "Okay, go ahead. I'll be the designated driver."

Virgil beamed. "Thanks, Dad."

"You boys do realize that there's not going to be any drinking once we start operation, since you'll be on call 24/7?"

"We know, Dad," Scott affirmed softly.

"I assume we can take a vacation once in a while," Virgil said.

"In rotation, yes," Jeff said, nodding.

They gave their orders. Jeff ordered black coffee and a t-bone, well done. Scott ordered a baked potato and a sirloin, medium, with a Milwaukee beer. Virgil ordered prime rib and french fries with a Colorado beer. John ordered a rib eye with Texas toast and a Canadian beer. Brains ordered a porterhouse steak and au gratin potatoes with a Guinness. They all ordered the house salad as an appetizer.

As they waited for the food to arrive, they noticed that they could see—and hear—the main cook, a large burly man, grilling away in the back. The server addressed him as "Dad." They also saw televisions hung from the ceilings, showing a racing event. Suddenly, Alan's face appeared on the screen.

"I'm just a spectator here," Alan said to the reporter.

"Are you sure you're not thinking of entering a race?" the reporter persisted.

Alan chuckled amiably. "Oh, I might think about it."

"Good for him!" the cook commented. "It's about time one of those Tracy boys broke away from the old man. They used to be their own men, and now that old geezer is hoarding them like a dragon hoards gold. He's going to ruin those boys, mark my word. They'll be good for nothing but sitting on the beach sipping martinis."

"Some p-p-people have t-t-too much time on their hands," Brains murmured.

"Don't let it bother you, boys," Jeff said softly. "He's not saying anything that the whole world isn't saying."

John sighed and shrugged. "It's good for our cover, I guess."

Scott looked around. "I think that lady in the blue jeans is giving you the eye, Virgil."

Virgil glanced up. "Are you sure she's not looking at you?"

"Well, the lady in the jumpsuit wearing the tool belt is smiling at Brains," John said.

"Me?" Brains raised his head and turned. Sure enough, the woman waved at him. Brains waved back politely and took another sip of his Guinness.

"The gray-haired one over there is flirting with Dad," Scott said.

Jeff chuckled. "Not my type, though. I think the one in the green pantsuit is checking John out."

"We're all the center of attention today, I guess," Scott said. "Too bad we don't have the time to go out for a dance or two."

Jeff checked his watch. "Afraid not, boys."

When they finished, Jeff went to the checkout counter and handed the server his bill—where he had written in a generous tip—and his cash card. She put the card through and looked at it. "Oh, my gosh," she breathed.

The cook looked over from his grilling. "Something wrong?"

"No, I just gave her a nice tip," Jeff said, taking a toothpick from the cup and unwrapping it. "My compliments to the chef. It was a great meal." The others murmured assent.

"Y'all come back, hear?" the cook called.

"If we can."

The server leaned over and whispered, "Sorry, Mr. Tracy."

Jeff waved a dismissal. "No problem. You've got a nice place here."

Once they were out the door, Scott said to Jeff, "You think she'll tell him?"

Jeff used the toothpick and answered, "I think he knew who I was when I walked in the door."

"Well, I'll be," John said. "That was bold of him."

"It's a free country," Jeff said, unflustered.

When they got back to Tracy Island, Jeff went to his quarters and checked the Internet news reports, as was his habit. Seeing a startling item, he folded his laptop and went to search for Kyrano. He found him tending this garden; the plants already had started to sprout in the rich volcanic soil. Jeff knelt beside Kyrano and opened the laptop. "Have you seen this?"

Kyrano read the screen. "I had thought my brother was still in jail in Canada."

"Apparently he was arrested in Thailand two days ago and just escaped there."

"I see."

"Kyrano...Honolulu is between Canada and Thailand. I can't help but wonder if he had something to do with Gordon's accident."

"I cannot say, Jeff Tracy."

"Nor can I. It could have been just a mechanical failure. But I think we're going to have to be careful from now on about going places where our presence is announced well in advance. That goes for Tin-Tin as well as the boys."

Kyrano nodded. "I think you are right."

Putting together the pods and auxiliary vehicles took a lot less time than constructing the hangars, largely because they only had to adapt existing technology for their purposes. The only exception was the drilling vehicle which the Tracys quickly named "The Mole." Nothing remotely like it existed in the world outside Tracy Island, so it had to be built largely "from scratch."

The assembly process, at first, seemed fairly straightforward. At the direction of Brains, they laid out all the components on the floor of the main hangar under the Cliff House. Then they used the diagrams Brains provided to put them together. One day, however, John and Brains approached Jeff with solemn expressions.

Jeff looked up from his console, set up at a corner of the hangar. "What's up, boys?"

"We have a p-p-problem, Mr. Tracy."

John put a foot up on one of the crates they used to sit on and leaned toward Jeff. "The intake we have for the reactor won't work."

Jeff leaned back slightly. "How could that happen?"

Brains sighed. "Because we wanted what we're doing to be secret, I c-c-couldn't be too specific, or someone might deduce what it was for. As a result, the part is what I described, but not what I wanted."

"I see." Jeff scratched his chin. "Can we adapt the part we did get for our purposes?"

John shook his head. "We tried."

"Well, what can we do?"

"I don't know, Mr. Tracy. I can give a manufacturer a detailed circuit diagram, but then how would we keep it a secret?"

Jeff smiled wryly. "Secret, eh? I think I know where we can get some help."

8

Lady Penelope Creighton-Ward looked up at the coat of arms in the drawing room and sighed. The Creighton-Wards had served the crown for centuries: the family motto was "Elegance, Charm, and Deadly Danger." Penelope, as with many of her forebears, had enlisted in the secret service, and risen up the ranks. Suddenly, however, she found herself dismissed and out of a job, not because of anything she did, but because her superiors had heard that certain elements on the Other Side had pursued an investigation of her—not as an agent, but as the international celebrity figure she used as a cover. If they persisted, her superiors feared that her true occupation would be exposed, which would compromise all sorts of state secrets. As a result, her services would no longer be required.

Penelope felt it was all rubbish, and had said so. She felt confident enough in her abilities that the Other Side could not touch her, much less expose her. But the decision had gone all the way up to the Prime Minister's office, and, in the end, she had to accept it.

Life since then had been a bit of a bore...or, in truth, more than a bore. But the Fates seemed to have discerned her desire, and had provided her with a new assignment: International Rescue. Jeff Tracy, who appeared to have his own means of getting information, had approached her and asked if she would be "on call," so to speak, to help him when needed.

Even further, the Fates had provided her with a new partner: Aloysius "Nosey" Parker, a felon and expert safecracker who had served his time and now sought to make an honest living in her service. At present, he was taking advanced courses in defensive/evasive driving as part of his bodyguard training. Prior to that, he had graduated from a school of estate management—in earlier times, this had been known as becoming a butler. Initially, Penelope had felt a twinge of doubt as to whether Parker could get through this training, given his background, but the instructors had told her that Parker had been a model student. This, if nothing else, reassured her that she had made the right choice and that Parker had indeed given up his life of crime.

Her cell phone beeped. No ordinary phone, it sent and received an encrypted signal. Only one person would be calling on that phone: Jeff Tracy.

She took it out. "Yes, Jeff, what can I do for you?"

"Are you alone, Penny?"

"Yes, Jeff," she said, looking around forlornly at the empty room. "Quite alone."

"I need you for an important task."

"I'm at your service, Jeff."

Jeff explained the problem, as Brains had given it to him.

"I think I know who can help. Do you know Sir Jeremy Hodge?"

"Why, yes," Jeff said, sounding surprised. "I talked to him about International Rescue. He said that his experiments with advanced rocket fuels wouldn't allow him to help me directly, but he wished me well. I didn't know you knew him."

Penelope smiled. "If it involves top secret projects, I know about it. And Sir Jeremy's work is top secret."

"How could he help?"

"He works with factories all over Europe. Factories which provide technology for secret government projects. The workers are all sworn not to divulge what they've worked on."

"I wouldn't want to work with any shady outfits."

"Oh, no, they're strictly legitimate. But no one knows about them except the governments involved. What I was thinking was that Sir Jeremy could order the parts you need, and everyone would think it was for his research."

"Wouldn't someone examining his financial transactions know he did it for us?"

"Sir Jeremy uses his own private funds for certain projects. As long as a government isn't paying for it, no one will bother to trace it."

"That sounds perfect. Can you arrange that, Penny?"

"Yes, but you'll have to provide Sir Jeremy with the part specifications."

Countdown to Action! 105

"I'll have Brains transmit the information in an encrypted databurst. Just have Sir Jeremy get in touch with us."

"I will."

"...no trouble at all," Sir Jeremy said when Jeff explained the problem. "Happy to help. After looking at the plans your assistant sent, I know precisely the firms that you need."

"And everything will be secret?" Jeff asked.

"No one will be the wiser," Sir Jeremy explained. "I order all sorts of technology for my work. They'll think it's Sir Jeremy up to his old tricks."

"How about payment?" Jeff asked.

"They send the invoices electronically. I can forward them to you."

John moved forward so that the was in view of the webcam on Jeff's desktop, which Jeff had used to call Sir Jeremy. "If you can trust us with your bank account numbers and access codes, I can transfer the money from our account to yours and then yours to the manufacturers'."

"Of course I trust you chaps," Sir Jeremy said. "You're taking a far greater risk than I am."

"We're in your debt, Sir Jeremy," Jeff said. "Thank you."

"You're welcome," Sir Jeremy said. "Exciting stuff you're working on. I only wish I'd thought of it myself. If I wasn't deep into my own work, I might be tempted to rush over there and join you."

Once Jeff ended the conversation, the others gathered around. "What do we do in the meantime?" Scott asked.

"There's no lack of work to do," Jeff said. "We haven't installed the power plant yet, or the waste treatment plant, or the water purification plant. There's the monorail connecting the hangars to be built, and we can start the excavation for the foundation of the house."

Virgil rubbed his hands together. "Let's get to it."

Without Gordon or Alan, the work on Tracy Island proceeded more slowly, but it did proceed. One day, when Jeff was washing up before lunch, his cell phone rang. The boys, also washing up at the lavatory in the barge, leaned over to see the caller ID on the laptop, which was linked to the cell phone.

"Dad, it's the rehab center," John called.

"I hope Gordon's all right," Scott said.

"He was doing so well when we saw him last Sunday," Virgil added.

Jeff sat at the desk and took the call at the laptop. The rehab center's administrator came on the screen.

"Mr. Tracy, we have a problem with Gordon."

"Now, Ms. Baker, we already told Gordon he was not to make squirt guns and smuggle them to the children's ward anymore."

"It isn't that, Mr. Tracy," Baker complained. "We started water therapy today, and he won't get out of the pool."

Brains and the Tracy sons started to chuckle. Jeff waved at them to be quiet; they covered their mouths. "How long has he been in there?"

"Three hours, Mr. Tracy. We've tried everything, but he just won't come out."

"Oh, he'll come out. He always comes out to eat. Go to that food storage unit that we put in his room and take out the bag of jelly beans. Tell him if he doesn't come out, you'll lock them away where he can't get them. Then give it to him when he does come out. That oughta do it."

"Okay, Mr. Tracy. We'll try it."

When Jeff terminated the call, the boys burst out in laughter. Jeff chuckled himself. "At least that means he's getting better."

As was Jeff's custom, he brought the laptop to the lunch table. After finishing his coffee and one of Kyrano's melt-in-your-mouth puff pastries, the laptop rang again.

"You're popular today, Father," Scott observed from across the lunch table.

Jeff opened the laptop and activated the connection.

Sir Jeremy's face popped up. "Everything's at my lab. Did you want it sent by special courier?"

"No," Jeff said firmly. "I'll come and pick it up myself."

"No trouble to leave it here a while," Sir Jeremy offered.

"It won't take that long," Jeff said, "I'll take the helijet to Hilo, and then a Tracy Technologies cargo jet to England. I'll be there in about twelve hours."

Countdown to Action! 107

"I'll be waiting."

Jeff terminated the call and turned to his middle son. "Okay, John, time to pay the invoices."

John took a seat next to his father, as Jeff slid the desktop to him. After using the touchpad, three windows appeared on the screen. Pointing to them, he said to Jeff, "Those are the invoices, that's our bank account, and that's Sir Jeremy's."

Jeff put a finger to the screen. "Those are our current liquid assets?"

"Yes. Enough, but the payments will deplete them by more than 50 percent. On the other hand, the interest on the CDs and other investments will make up for that in six months to a year."

"I don't expect any other major payments between now and then, and if they come up, we can transfer some of the principal," Jeff said. Seeing his other sons get up from the lunch table, he called to them. "It wouldn't hurt you two to learn the financial side of our operations."

Scott turned to Virgil, and then back to Jeff. "Spreadsheets make my eyes glaze over."

Jeff turned to John, then back to his other sons. "Okay, then. Just get the helijet ready for take off."

"That we can do!" Virgil said enthusiastically. He left with Scott.

Meanwhile, John took out his own PDA and consulted some numbers there. Entering them on the keypad, he said, "Okay. I'm transferring our funds to Sir Jeremy's account." He paused a short time, and looked at the screen with Sir Jeremy's assets. "There they are," he said, as they were credited. He entered more numbers. "Now they're going from Sir Jeremy's account to the various manufacturers. There's one invoice paid…two… uh-huh…. Okay, they're all paid."

Jeff stood and patted John on the shoulder. "Good work, John. I knew I could count on you."

"Call for you, Alan. It's your brother, Gordon."

Alan got up from the couch in the living room where he had been playing a video game with Kenny until the telecall rang. Kenny had answered the phone in the kitchen and now walked past Alan as Alan went to take the call.

Gordon's face showed on the screen. His laptop had been enabled to send and receive calls; Alan could see the wall of the rehab center room in the background.

"Alan!" he said excitedly. "I can swim!"

Alan's thought was that for Gordon, that was like saying "fish can swim." Instead, he said blandly, "That's great, Gordon."

"Aw, c'mon, Alan. That means I'm getting better!"

"I knew you were better when you told me that you had made and provided a water pistol for every kid in the children's wing."

"It got them up and moving. Good for their morale."

Alan chuckled. "Yeah, and it got a lot of doctors and physical therapists soggy, too."

"Speaking of which, the physical therapist says maybe I could leave in just another couple of weeks."

"Where will you go then?"

Gordon inhaled in surprise. "Back to the island, of course, silly!"

"You don't have to, you know."

"I guess I don't have to. But I want to."

"Your funeral...."

"You make it sound so depressing! I was having fun. Weren't you?"

"No. Dad was on my back from the start. It was almost as if he was trying to make me leave...like he didn't want me. And that stuff I told you about him 'training' us to be his aides was just the last straw."

"He was making us all work hard, Alan, but he wasn't working any less hard than we were. Yeah, he yells a lot, but that's just how he is. He's always been that way, in case you haven't noticed. And he leveled with us right from the start: he told us he'd be in charge and we'd have to follow his orders. I didn't expect this to be a walk in the park."

"Sure, but he also told us there would be all these wonderful...," Alan glanced back to the living room, trying to determine whether Kenny might be able to hear, "...rewards. I didn't see any."

Gordon sighed. "You're just too impatient, Alan. But the others have told me, confidentially, that they're just on the verge of the, uh, rewards. So you could come back and be right in the middle of the action."

"I'm not coming back; not, at least, until I get an apology from Father."

"For what?" Gordon asked, sounding genuinely puzzled. "I mean, Dad's always been pretty strict, but he's never crossed the line."

"It doesn't bother you that he's been training us all our lives just to serve him? He's always getting his way, and we have to pay for it!"

"Are you kidding, Alan? Get his way? If he'd been getting his way, I wouldn't have had to remind him that he promised Mom that he'd let me join the aquanauts instead of going to college. Besides, he gave us all a choice...to join him or walk away."

"Well, that's what I did. I walked away."

"Your loss, Alan."

"I'm doing just fine here, thank you."

"Fine, huh? Enter any races lately?"

Alan shrugged. "I'm looking around. Been to some."

"Uh-huh." He paused and looked around. "Well, the physical therapist is coming back. Gotta go."

"I'm glad you're better, Gordon. Really."

"Oh, I know. Right now, I wonder if you're in worse shape than me. Bye." The screen went blank.

"What?" Alan said to the screen, startled. He shook his head and went back to the living room, where he sat on the couch next to Kenny. Taking his video game control, he said, "Now, where were we?"

Once Jeff reached England, and securely stored the parts in the Tracy Technologies cargo jet, he accepted Sir Jeremy's invitation to stay with him for the night. The flight from Tracy Island had been long, and Jeff found it more difficult at his age to stay up for 24 hours straight than he had when he was younger. After a good night's rest, and after taking the latest over-the-counter medications for jet lag, he felt much better. Sir Jeremy offered to take Jeff to the Rolls Royce factory, where his host took a moment to admire the specially-built car that Jeff picked up and purchased before going back to his lab.

Jeff drove the Rolls directly to the gates of Creighton Manor. When a short man wearing a double-breasted uniform and cap answered the ring at the door, Jeff said, "You must be Parker."

Parker looked to be about Jeff's age, though he was significantly shorter. His cap largely covered his gray hair and sideburns. The bridge of his nose, which was above the level of his eyes, protruded from his forehead between two bushy eyebrows. "And you must be Mr. Tracy. Come in, sir, her ladyship is expecting you."

Jeff smiled. "Have her ladyship come out here."

"As you wish, sir." He disappeared.

About a minute later, Penelope walked out on the front step. Seeing the huge, pink Rolls Royce parked in the driveway, she exclaimed, "Why, Jeff, it's fabulous!"

"It ought to be," Jeff said, strolling toward the car. Penelope followed Jeff; Parker followed her. "It's armored and bulletproof. The transparent canopy here is also bulletproof. The tires," he kicked one of the four front tires, "can't be punctured." He opened the door so the two could see the control panel. "And there's an assortment of weaponry."

"Shall I take it out for a spin?" Penelope asked.

"I'd let Parker do the driving." Jeff took out the keys and handed them to the chauffeur.

Penelope crossed her arms in front of her. "Jeff, I can drive, you know."

"This is no ordinary car, Penny. It takes special training to drive a car like this." Jeff nodded to Parker. "Parker's had that training at that driving school you sent him to."

"Very well," Penelope said. "Parker, take Mr. Tracy's bags."

Parker reached inside and took the handle of Jeff's suitcase from the back seat. "There's more in the trunk," Jeff told him.

"Do you have a key for the boot?" Penelope asked.

Jeff flipped a switch on the driver's panel. "You open it from here."

Between Jeff and Parker, they carried all of Jeff's bags and boxes inside. "Some of these I want you to see right away," Jeff said.

Penelope motioned. "Come right into the drawing room." Turning to Parker he added, "Take Mr. Tracy's other bags to the guest room."

"Yes, m'lady."

Jeff took two large boxes and one small box with him and followed Penelope. She led the way to the drawing room and shut the door. As he set the boxes on the floor, a portrait of Penelope caught his eye. The stately blonde wore a fox chasing—it used to be "fox hunting" until laws had been passed against it—outfit, showing off her slim figure.

"Have a seat," Penelope said.

Jeff sat on the couch opposite Penelope's chair. He placed a box on a low table in front of him and opened it, taking out a silver tea service.

"Why, Jeff, it's lovely...but I already have a silver tea service."

"I know, but not like this one." He twisted the top of the tea pot. "This is a communication device."

"Really?" Penelope said, leaning forward with interest.

He spoke into it. "Jeff Tracy to base."

After a short pause, they could hear John's voice. "Reading you five by five, Dad."

"That's my son, John," Jeff said in a low voice. In a louder voice, he added, "Just testing the communications signal I gave to Penelope."

"Okay, Dad. Everything's fine here. Anything else?"

"No, I've got the parts we need and should be back there in the next couple of days. I'm just here to get Penelope set up."

"Give her our regards. We're all anxious to meet her in person."

Penelope leaned forward. "And I'm anxious to meet all of you. Jeff has told me so much about you."

"And Dad's told us all about you and Parker."

"All in good time," Jeff said. "Right now we need to concentrate on our respective tasks. Thanks, John. I'll talk to you later."

"Right, Dad. Over and out."

"This is just fabulous, Jeff. Much more than I ever imagined."

"You're going to need all the right equipment to give us a hand." He patted the other large box on the floor. "I've got more installation to do." He touched the smaller box. "And here are some portable communication devices for when you're out in the field."

"This is even better than when I was working secretly for the government."

Jeff smiled. "You're working secretly for us, now."

With Penelope watching, Jeff took off his jacket, rolled up his sleeves, and took out the communications devices from the small box. After he explained and demonstrated them to Penelope, he asked her where to install the video screen. Penelope explained that the mansion already had extensive audio and video monitors installed for security. Jeff found an outlet he could use and took out his power tools. While she watched, he noisily installed Brains's devices, which neatly fit with the existing structure.

"This is all fabulous," she said as she watched over Jeff's shoulder.

"What?" he called, continuing his work.

"Fabulous," she called back, in a louder voice.

"What?"

"Fabulous."

"What?"

"F-A-B...." She stopped spelling when he turned off the power tool.

Jeff looked at her curiously. "Fabulous," he whispered.

"Yes. F-A-B-U-L-O-U-S. Fabulous."

"F-A-B," he said.

"Yes, fab, like the famous rock group."

He turned and leaned back against the wall. "You know, Penny, I've been thinking that we need a code word to identify ourselves on our own communications channels, something that no one else would use. I think that would work just fine."

"What would?"

"F.A.B."

She inhaled sharply. "Yes, Jeff, what a fabulous...I mean... what an F.A.B. idea!"

He chuckled. "I think you've got it, Penny!"

Alan and Kenny decided to go fishing. They checked the weather forecast; the day was predicted to be sunny and hot. Kenny led the way to the pier where his 30-foot fishing boat was docked, after they coated themselves with an all-day sunscreen. As they stepped in with their fishing equipment and their cooler of food and drinks, Alan pointed to what appeared to be an old-fashioned riverboat, an enormous two-story rectangular craft complete with paddlewheel.

"What's that?"

"Oh, that's a casino boat. It travels up and down the west coast of Florida."

"How long will it stay?"

"It generally docks a week or two before moving on."

"Ever been on it?"

"Oh, yeah. They have stage plays and live jazz bands and comedy acts as well as gambling."

"Sounds interesting. Think we could go sometime, maybe Saturday?"

"Nah, Saturday's too crowded. Tuesday's the best day to go."

"How about it?"

"Sure. But let's get some fish first."

Alan chuckled. "Okay!" he said enthusiastically.

Kenny started the boat and consulted the GPS on board to get the bearings he needed to get to his favorite fishing spot. Alan sat in a cushioned seat on the side of the boat, wearing a lightweight orange life vest over a green t-shirt and swim trunks. At first, Kenny drove slowly around the other boats near the harbor. As they increased their distance from the shore, the number of boats around them decreased. Kenny pushed the velocity lever forward and soon it seemed they were skipping along the ocean's surface. Eventually, Alan noticed they were out of sight of the shore. Not long after that, Alan turned and found no other boats in sight.

Throughout the ride, Kenny looked from the GPS to the water and steered accordingly. Finally, he slowed to a stop. He touched a control. "Dropping the anchor," he explained. He consulted another monitor, turned, and smiled at Alan. "The sonar says there are fish nearby!"

"Okay!" Alan said, rising from his seat and reaching for his fishing rod. "We're in business!"

They brought ample supplies: an ice chest filled with bottled juices and soft drinks; another refrigerated chest with sandwiches they could heat in the boat's small microwave; a large box with bags of snacks. Another refrigerated chest, now empty, would hold the fish they caught.

The two young men cast out their lines and settled back. While waiting for a fish to bite, they talked and started on the snacks and drinks. By noon, Kenny had three "keepers" and Alan had two, though they had caught and released several smaller fish.

Kenny shaded his eyes and turned toward the sun, high in the sky. "What do you think, Alan? Do you want to go back, or fish some more?"

"It's all the same to me, Kenny. Whatever you want."

"Okay. Let's troll for a bit. I'll point the boat toward shore, lock the rudder, and the engine will just inch us forward slowly. We can cast our lines out the back."

At first, Kenny and Alan glanced to the bow frequently, but with no other boats in the area, they did so less and less. Suddenly, the engine made a high-pitched noise, sputtered, and ground to a halt.

"What was that?" Alan asked.

Kenny leaned out and said, "Oh, no!"

Alan looked in that direction. A big mass of green, floating on the surface, surrounded the boat. "Seaweed?" Alan speculated.

Kenny sat down and sighed. "Partly. Remember in the old days how people would just dump trash into the ocean? Well, it's been sitting there for decades, and meanwhile it's collected seaweed and algae and dead fish and old fishing nets and all sorts of junk. Every once in a while, a trawler or submarine will dislodge a piece and it'll float to the surface. Eventually it breaks up and sinks again, but until then it's a hazard."

"And we ran into it."

"Yeah. And it got into the engine intake."

"Can we clear it?"

"Maybe. I can take a look. Sometimes you can. Otherwise, we'll just have to call a boat towing service to come and pick us up."

"There are boat towing services?"

"Sure. Just like when your car stalls on the side of the road. Happens all the time."

Kenny lifted the engine cap on the deck and looked down. He reached for the toolkit and got a flashlight. "Well, I can see where it's clogged. If nothing else is tangled in there, I think I can reach in and get it out."

"I wouldn't want the engine to shear off your hand. Maybe we should just call the towing service."

"No, there's a safety catch there." He handed the flashlight to Alan and pointed. "Just shine it there. I'll reach in."

Kenny lay on the deck on his stomach and reached in. "Okay. I think I got it...I think I got it...I think I... argh!" He shouted in pain as the boat suddenly lurched. Kenny's arm, stuck in the hole, was nearly wrenched from the socket.

"Kenny!" Alan said in alarm. He knelt and gently pulled out Kenny's arm. The hand and wrist seemed fine. Kenny, however, sat on the deck, grimacing in pain. "It's the shoulder!" he said. "I think it's dislocated."

Alan knelt and as gently as he could, rolled up the short sleeve of Kenny's t-shirt. The shoulder did look funny, exactly as if something was out of place.

"Alan," Kenny croaked, his left hand gingerly touching his injured right shoulder. "Do something...please."

"I think we better get to shore and get you to a hospital."

"No! Do it now!"

Alan sighed. "All right. I was trained for this on a dummy as a paramedic, though I hadn't done it for real." He got Kenny to lay flat. Then he braced his foot against Kenny's shoulder, took Kenny's right hand in his, and moved the arm back and forth. Soon, Kenny nodded. "Yeah! That's it! But man, it hurts!"

Alan moved to the ice chest. "I'm going to pack it in ice. Do you have a first aid kit?"

"Yeah. Under the driver's seat."

As Alan moved, Kenny painfully climbed onto the bench on the port side of the boat. Alan found the first aid kit, some wraps, a blanket, and a pillow. He put the ice in the wraps, secured the shoulder, and got Kenny settled. There was aspirin in the kit, and he gave Kenny that, too—it was better than nothing.

"I think we need to call for a tow." Alan said when Kenny seemed to be reclining comfortably.

Kenny motioned with his good arm. "There's a radio on the dashboard."

Alan slid into the driver's seat and activated the radio. "This is boat FLA28927," he said, reading the ID letters on the dash, "calling Tampa Bay Towing Service. Come in." Seconds passed, nothing. Alan repeated the call. Still nothing. He turned to Kenny. "Is the radio working?"

Kenny groaned. "There's probably sharp stuff in with the junk that cut the battery cable. Take my cell phone from my pack over there. It's on the speed dial."

Alan found it easily and dialed. "Busy."

"Busy?"

Alan sighed. "I guess I can try the Coast Guard." After he dialed, he heard. "Coast Guard. What is your emergency?"

"I'm in a boat offshore with a friend. The boat's engine is disabled and we're floating free. My friend dislocated his shoulder. We need help."

"Is your friend stable?"

"Yes. I fixed it temporarily, but he's in pain, of course. He needs a doctor to look at it."

"Is your boat sinking?"

"No, we're fine, as far as that goes."

"Then I'll put you on our call list, but it's going to take a while to get to you. The casino boat caught fire, and all emergency agencies have their hands full."

"That's horrible! Are there casualties?"

"It's a full scale disaster. You're lucky to have reached me at all. We can't possibly take a non-emergency call."

"Okay. I guess I understand."

"I have your cell GPS. I've made a note of where you are. I'll send someone when someone's available. Coast Guard out."

"Wow," Kenny said, "it must be really bad out there."

"Yeah," Alan said glumly. "I guess I do understand that they have to take care of the fire."

"Well, it isn't as if I'm dying or anything."

Alan looked eastward. He pointed. "Look, there's smoke on the horizon over there."

Kenny turned his head. "Yeah, it must be really bad if we can see it from here."

Alan sat across from Kenny. The boat lurched again. He leaned over the side. "What the heck is going on?"

"Dunno," Kenny said from his reclining position.

Alan held up a hand. "Wait. Hear that noise?"

Countdown to Action! 117

They both held their breaths. A low bellowing sound reached their ears; then they heard a snort.

Alan leaned over to the other side. "There's a manatee there, Kenny, tangled in an old net."

"He's far from home. They rarely go more than a mile from shore. Current probably carried him out here."

"Well, he seems to be...," Alan caught the side of the boat as it lurched again, "...rubbing against the boat to try to get free from it."

"That explains it," Kenny said. "Those manatees can weigh half a ton."

"It's a big fellow, all right," Alan affirmed. "I wish Gordon was here; he'd know what to do."

"Well, the wildlife service says leave them alone if you see them. You might do him more harm than good if you try to help him."

"I can't reach him, anyway." He sat next to Kenny.

Kenny's cell phone had games on it; he and Alan amused themselves for an hour. Just to be sure they were really stranded, Alan checked the engine himself. He took a long rod and used that to poke around, but it soon became clear that the clog Kenny saw was only part of the problem. The sludge and debris had inundated the engine. It would have to be taken apart and rebuilt before it would ever work again.

Another hour passed. "Let's try emergency services again," Alan suggested. "Maybe the disaster area is secure by now."

"Here, use my cell phone." He extended his free arm to give it to Alan, but the boat rocked again, Kenny's arm snapped back, and the cell phone flipped into the ocean.

"No!" Alan called, and leaned over the side. The cell phone was gone. "Darn manatee!"

"He's stuck just as we are," Kenny explained.

Alan sighed. He sat purposefully on the deck, well away from the water, and took out his own cell phone. He looked at the cell phone screen. "Oh, great!"

"What is it?"

"Battery's low."

"Well, go ahead and try someone before it goes out completely."

Alan tried universal 911, emergency services: nothing. In desperation, he went to the phone directory and hit the first number that came up: DAD. "Argh! I got the message machine!"

"Then leave a message."

"Okay. Dad, if you can hear this, this is Alan. Kenny and I are in a boat west of Tampa Bay. The engine's fried. We can't get emergency services because there's a disaster in Tampa Bay. The boat's adrift, and Kenny's arm is dislocated. If you can call anybody, please do." He looked at the readout again.

"Did you get through?"

Alan shook his head. "No idea. The screen's gone dark."

"I guess we just wait, then."

"Yeah, but how long?"

9

At three o'clock, Alan leaned over the side again. "I'm going to see if I can help the manatee. I have nothing else to do."

"Careful," Kenny said.

"I will be." There was a seat with straps on it, in case they wanted to try to catch a marlin or other large fish. Alan secured himself and got a long rod with a small hook on the end. It took several tries, but he finally snagged the net with the hook and dragged it off the manatee. "There you are, big fella," he said, as the manatee snorted its relief at being free. Then it dipped under the water, surfaced away from the floating seaweed, and swam off.

"At least he'll get home," Kenny said as Alan unstrapped himself and put the rod back in its place. "Too bad he couldn't carry a message to the Coast Guard for us."

"Yeah, that only happens in the movies," Alan said. "But someone will come," he added with more optimism than he felt.

When Alan sat beside him again, Kenny said, "You know, there ought to be a rescue service just for people to call when the regular rescue guys can't come."

Alan sat glumly staring at the deck.

Kenny raised his head from where he was reclining. "Alan?"

"Sorry, I'm just...frustrated."

"Yeah, so am I."

By four o'clock, all the ice in the chest was gone. Alan had wrapped Kenny's shoulder about 3 times, and then the ice would melt and he would get more ice and wrap it again. Kenny claimed, though, that as long as he did not move, the shoulder did not bother him anymore.

They drank the juices first and those were gone by the time the ice was. The soft drinks would keep; they might not taste as well warm but they would not spoil. When the refrigerated chest started getting warm, they ate the sandwiches. The bags of snacks in the box would stay fresh until the bags were opened.

"We ought to have some help before everything's gone," Kenny said, as he brushed crumbs off his shirt with his good arm.

"We ought to have had some help a long time ago," Alan insisted. "Where are they?"

"Maybe the Coast Guard dispatcher lost the note."

"Well, we can't just sit here!"

"I'm game for trying anything Alan, but what? We can't row. We can't take the engine out and fix it, not with the tools we have."

"Can we rig a sail?" Alan asked.

"We have all sorts of rods and there are plenty of blankets and beach towels."

"I'll try it, then."

Making a sail proved to be a difficult task. Even with all the various rods and ropes and blankets, Alan could not make a stable frame. Whenever he thought he had a sturdy frame, attempting to tie the blankets to it caused the frame to collapse. Alan cut strips from the blankets, poked holes near the edges, and tried to secure the blankets to the frames with the strips. Then the holes would widen and rip to the edges. Kenny tried to help, using his good arm to hold things steady while Alan worked, but in the end, nothing worked.

In frustration, Alan threw a rod against the side of the boat. "Argh!"

Kenny sighed. "What time is it?"

Alan sat and looked at his watch. "About a quarter past six." He looked to the western horizon. "When does the sun set?"

"I don't know, but it's getting low, isn't it?"

Alan sighed. "I guess we have to think about staying here overnight." He looked around the boat. "Do you have flares?"

Kenny pointed with his good arm.

"Okay, found them." Alan took them out.

"I wouldn't use them unless you actually see an aircraft."

"I won't."

Kenny rubbed his forehead.

"You okay?"

"Yeah. Just tired. I think I'll take a nap."

"I dunno, Kenny...."

"C'mon, Alan. I don't have a concussion, I'm not shivering. I'm just tired."

Alan looked at Kenny with his paramedic's eye. It was true: Kenny was not pale, his skin was not clammy, his mental function was fine. "Okay, but if it looks to me as if something's wrong, I'm waking you up."

"Fair enough." Kenny pulled the blanket closer and settled on the bench.

Alan found he did not need to worry. Every 10 or 20 minutes, Kenny would shift position, move his legs or arms to get more comfortable, or just wave at him.

Meanwhile, Alan sat on the other side of the boat, watching as the sun sank lower and lower. He scanned from horizon to horizon and shook his head. Wasn't anyone coming? Didn't anyone care? He rubbed his scalp with his fingers, mussing his hair. Finally, he began to sob. He tried to be quiet about it, so Kenny would not hear, but the tears flowed and he used a handkerchief to wipe his face.

When he calmed down, he looked up at the clear sky. *If I ever get out of this*, he told himself, *I'm going back to Tracy Island if I have to crawl. I'll mop the floors and clean the toilets if I have to, but I will not let anyone else have to go through this if I can help it!*

The sky seemed to be going dim. Looking west, he saw the sun had just disappeared below the water. He began to look around the boat to see if he could salvage any of the blankets he tried to fashion sails of, so he could make a bed for himself. He glanced toward Kenny to check on him, and in so doing, spotted a star in the east. Venus? John would know, he did not. But it was bright, and it was moving...faster than a planet. An aircraft?

Quickly, he found the flare gun. Pointing it upward, he fired. For the first time that day, it seemed, something worked—the flare rose perfectly, burst, and glowed brightly. Alan kept watching the light. It came closer. He saw it blink on and off. He fired off another flare, and waited. Now he could hear the engines.

In the twilight, he saw the outline of a helijet headed toward them. It turned on a searchlight.

Kenny wakened. "What's going on?"

"It's a helijet!" Alan breathed. "It looks like someone's come at last!" He had to shield his eyes from the brightness as a figure descended, let down from the helijet by a cable. The figure wore a helmet with the visor down. When the figure's feet were at the level of Alan's head, he reached up to pull the rescuer onto the deck.

"Are you all right, Alan?" said a familiar voice. The helmet came off.

"Dad!" Alan said, astonished, as his father embraced him.

When Jeff released Alan, he repeated, "Are you all right?"

"Yeah. Kenny's shoulder is dislocated."

Jeff turned to Kenny.

"Hi, Mr. Tracy."

Jeff wore an earpiece with a microphone. "Lower a stretcher."

When they were all in the helijet and Kenny was secure in the back being examined by the Tracy Technologies doctor, Alan said to Jeff, "How did you find me?"

"I got your phone message just seconds after you hung up. I was in the shower when the message came. I tried calling you back, but there was no answer. I called the Tampa Bay area emergency services, but there was no answer. I was at Lady Penelope's mansion; the casino boat disaster was all over the TV. So she—or rather, her chauffeur—drove me to the airport and I flew the cargo jet to Florida. It takes a while to cross the Atlantic, even at supersonic speeds. Even while I was in the air, I kept trying to get anyone from the city of Tampa to Sarasota without success. I landed at the Tracy Technologies airstrip at Cocoa Beach and used the Tracy Technologies helijet to go to Tampa Bay. By that time, the disaster area was secure and I was able to get in to Coast Guard headquarters where someone finally remembered that you had called. They saved your GPS location at the time so I knew approximately where you were. And here I am."

Alan was seated next to Jeff; he reached over and hugged his Dad. "Thanks, Dad. I'm so sorry."

"Sorry for what?" Jeff asked when Alan released him. "You didn't do anything wrong; you just had an engine failure. Could happen to anyone."

"No, I'm sorry for doubting you."

Jeff smiled. "Oh, that."

"I'm going back with you, Dad. I'm going home."

"Are you sure you want to?" Jeff asked curiously.

Alan nodded. "Whatever it takes, whatever it costs, whatever I have to do, even if I have to scrub the toilets with a toothbrush, I'll do it. No one should have to go through what I just went through. I'm giving it 100 per cent."

Jeff hugged Alan firmly. "Welcome back, son."

They left Kenny in good shape. In a matter of hours, the hospital had treated and released him. Jeff enlisted a service to deliver meals and clean the house, and therapists to come to the house until Kenny was completely recovered. Jeff also contacted a towing service to get the boat. Then Jeff and Alan took the helijet back to Cocoa Beach. After a good night's sleep in a nearby hotel, they boarded the cargo jet and set course to Tracy Island, Jeff in the pilot's seat, Alan in the co-pilot's.

When they were on their way and could use the autopilot, Jeff turned to Alan. "Brains has given us new communications devices." He lifted his wrist, displaying a watch with a large face. "This is called a telecom. You can see it looks like an ordinary wrist watch, but we'll be using it to communicate. The face is actually a projection; when you talk into it the dial goes away and you can see the person talking to you in it. It's tied to our satellite station that Tracy Technologies has just finished. We can call each other from anywhere on the planet."

"You mean the satellite is ready to go?" Alan said, impressed.

"Not yet. All that Tracy Technologies can do is done. But we will need to go up there once the spaceship is built and put in our own equipment."

"How's that going?"

Jeff nodded towards the rear of the jet. "We couldn't start constructing those until we got the equipment that's back there. The scaffolding is up; each respective vehicle has to be built on its respective launch pad."

"Which one are we building first?" Alan asked.

"All at once. I want you boys to build your own vehicles so you know every inch of them. They'll have to be maintained and repaired. Scott's got the rocket reconnaissance aircraft; Virgil has the heavy rescue craft; you and John will work on the space vehicle, and I'll start work on the submarine until Gordon gets back."

"Seems I've missed a lot," Alan said apologetically.

"There's still a lot to do," Jeff assured him.

They set the cargo jet down at the Tracy Technologies airstrip in Hilo, then loaded the helijet and went back to the island. Alan looked out the window and saw a half-constructed house as Jeff guided the helijet into the barge's heliport.

To Alan's surprise and relief, his brothers greeted him with enthusiasm, embracing him and patting him on the back.

"All right," Jeff said amiably. "We're all glad Alan's back; let's get this equipment unloaded."

Alan did more than his share in storing the equipment. When done, he went to the main hangar and watched as Virgil, Scott, and John put the finishing touches on the machine they called the Mole. Then the others stood aside as Virgil happily started it up and got it moving on its tractor treads.

Brains spoke into his watch/telecom. "Try the borer, Virgil."

"Will do," came Virgil's voice.

The borer in front of the machine spun around.

"Okay," Brains said, and Virgil shut it down. Moments later, he stepped out of the machine to applause.

At their next meal, Jeff told them all about his visit to Penelope and suggested using "F.A.B." as a call sign.

"Yeah," John said approvingly, "No one else will use that!"

"Speaking of names," Scott said, "what are we going to name the birds?"

"Birds?" Alan said.

"That's Air Force slang for 'aircraft,'" Jeff explained. He turned to Scott. "I don't know…I've thought of them as Rescue 1 for the rocket reconnaissance machine, Rescue 2 for the heavy rescue craft, Rescue 3 for the rocket ship, and so forth."

"Sounds kind of bland to me," Virgil said.

"I'm open to ideas," Jeff said.

"Gordon once suggested we ought to call them 'Larry, Moe, and Curly.'" Virgil said.

Countdown to Action! 125

Jeff chuckled. "Gordon would."

"Tom, Dick, and Harry?" Alan volunteered.

"Nah," Scott said.

"Doesn't seem appropriate to call something 'Harry' when it's thundering above you at supersonic speed," John said.

Scott's head went up. "Yeah. Thunder." He and Jeff pointed to each other and said simultaneously, "Thunderbirds!"

Scott held up a hand. "I've got Thunderbird 1."

"Thunderbird 2," Virgil said.

"Thunderbird 3," John said.

"The submarine can be Thunderbird 4," Jeff said.

"And the satellite can be Thunderbird 5," Alan said.

"That seems to settle it," Jeff said.

The next Sunday, they made their usual visit to Gordon. Brains stayed behind on the island again; Kyrano went shopping; Jeff said he had to pick up a package from Grandma and other things.

When the Tracy brothers got to Gordon's room at the rehab center, they saw Gordon dressed in street clothes; the rehab center felt residents would have better morale if they were not in hospital gowns. Sam sat next to him at a table, folding paper airplanes. They all said "hi" and Virgil set down the box he carried; it had Kyrano's meals for Gordon for the next week.

"Thanks!" Gordon said appreciatively.

Alan stepped forward and extended a hand to Sam. "Sam, I wanted to apologize. I was out of line."

Sam turned to Alan, startled, then slowly held out his hand and shook Alan's. "Sure, I accept your apology, Alan. If it were my brother, I'd be sore, too."

John surveyed the table. "What's going on here?"

"Well," Gordon said, "one of the physical therapists thought it would help my fine motor skills to do some origami. While I was at it, I thought, why not fold paper airplanes? So I asked Sam, here, to get me some paper. I drew some folding lines on it and he took it to the printer. So we're folding some examples and then we'll take a bunch to the children's wing. Then they can take their origami figures and put them in the paper planes and fly them all over the building!"

"What does the staff think about that?" Scott asked.

Gordon grinned. "The staff keeps telling me they're going to throw me out, but they're just kidding. Actually, the physical therapists say the kids make better progress and are more engaged when they have something fun to do."

"I understand you're having your share of fun, too," Virgil said.

Gordon turned to him. "I've been working hard, too. I have three hours of physical therapy every day."

"He means outside of the pool, Gordon," Alan said, and his brothers chuckled.

"I mean out of the pool," Gordon said. "They have me walking around all over. I even go to the park outside by myself and read sometimes. It's been much easier since they took off the back brace."

"Feeling well now?" Scott asked.

"Yeah, the doc said I can go home soon."

"Good." Scott put a hand under Gordon's shoulder and lifted him up. "Since we're speaking of fun, let's have some fun."

"Can we take Gordon out of here?" John asked.

"We'll tell them we're headed for the park," Scott said. "You can come, too, Sam."

Sam smiled and shook his head. "As I told Gordon, I just stopped in for a few minutes. I have to get on a plane for the next show in San Diego. Tell you what, though—I'll deliver the paper planes on my way out." He gathered the papers. "Good luck, Gordon, and the rest of you, too."

The others said good-bye to Sam as he walked out. Then Scott took Gordon's arm and led him out.

"Where are we headed?" Alan asked.

Since Kyrano and Jeff had the rented van, Scott called for a taxi and they crowded in. Scott told the cab driver to stop at a gun range, where they rented guns and goggles and ear protectors.

Though the range had six firing positions, they all crowded around Gordon as he shot. He fired a couple of rounds, then put the gun on the shelf and turned to his brothers. "You know, I'm not going to collapse."

"Just wanted to be sure," Scott said, and they spread out.

Gordon shot a 65 out of 100 at first, but worked his way up to a 90 by the end of two hours. When the attendant handed him his last target, Gordon looked at it glumly. "Only a 90."

Alan lightly punched Gordon's arm. "Only a 90? I got an 85!"

Scott patted Gordon's shoulder. "You'll get back to 100 in no time. There's a firing range on the barge, and we're building one in the house, too."

When they returned to the rehab center, they found Gordon's packed bags outside his door. The room had been cleaned and seemed ready for someone else. "What's going on?" Scott said, peeking in.

"I have no idea," Gordon said.

Ms. Baker, the rehab administrator, walked up to Gordon and handed him a clipboard. "Here, sign this."

Gordon took it and read it. "What is it?"

"These are your discharge papers. Your doctor transmitted orders that you could leave at any time. Since you seem inclined to leave now, we're happy to see you on your way."

Alan put his hand to his mouth and turned away, stifling a chuckle.

Gordon grinned and took a pen to sign.

Baker took back the clipboard. "And don't let me see you back here again, young man!"

"No, ma'am!" Gordon said as she walked away.

"Hooray for Gordon!" Virgil said. He and Scott lifted Gordon up and carried him out on their shoulders. John took the box of Kyrano's meals and Alan took Gordon's bags. They followed their brothers.

Scott called Jeff on his cell phone to tell him that they would meet him and Kyrano at the helijet. When they got out of the taxi, Scott paid the driver as Jeff walked up to Gordon and carefully hugged him.

"Dad, I'm not going to break."

Jeff released him. "I still want you to take it easy for a while, son...."

"Aw, Dad...."

"I want to be sure you're in shape once we start."

"Dad," Gordon insisted. "I've been doing physical therapy for three hours a day, lifting hand and leg weights twice a day, and swimming a mile once a day. I'm fine!"

Jeff held up a finger. "When we get back to the island, you're still going to work three hours a day, lift weights twice a day, and swim a mile a day in the pool we built."

"I sure will!"

"Good," Virgil said. "I've been feeling lonely in the barge's weight room!"

"We don't need to pump iron," John said. "We've all been hauling our weight in construction materials all day, every day!"

"Yeah," Virgil teased, patting his stomach, "but just doing that won't give you those nice washboard abs."

"Gives you some nice biceps, though," Scott said, flexing his arm to demonstrate.

"Okay, boys," Jeff said, "you can use some of those muscles and help Kyrano and me get the crates on the helijet."

As his brothers moved to take the boxes, Gordon walked up to Kyrano. "Thanks for supplying me with all the delicious meals. The doctor said all that good solid nutrition definitely helped me heal faster."

Kyrano smiled. "I was happy to help. I am glad that you are better."

"Much better, thanks to you." Gordon said. He turned to assist his father and brothers, but found they had already taken charge of the cargo.

Once they got back to the island, they gave Gordon a tour of the hangars. In each hangar, pieces of that hangar's aircraft lay spread out on the floor. "We bring them in one s-s-section at a time," Brains explained.

When they reached the site where Jeff had started assembling the submarine, Gordon took his time examining every part. "Looks okay so far, Dad," he said.

"I take that as a great compliment," Jeff said.

"I'll take over from here, though."

Jeff cleared his throat. "All right, but I'll still stand by to help."

"Dad, I *can* do this myself," Gordon said, meeting Jeff's eye.

"None of us can do this all by ourselves," Jeff insisted gently. "We each need to take a turn helping the others, even though each of you has a primary assignment. We have to cross-train on the equipment, as well. If one of us gets sick or injured, another has to step in to pilot or repair the craft."

"Okay, that makes sense," Gordon said.

"Come and see Tracy Villa," Jeff said.

The walls and floors were bare, and there were no pieces of furniture, but the general structure had taken shape. They showed Gordon where his bedroom would be, where the kitchen was—Kyrano had already started moving in the appliances—and where the lounge was.

Scott walked to a wall and laid a hand on a panel. "This is on a turntable. I'll stand on this and it'll swing around to the Thunderbird 1 hangar."

Virgil pointed to another wall panel. "We're installing a chute here that'll take me to the Thunderbird 2 hangar."

"There will also be an e-e-elevator to that hangar," Brains added.

Jeff indicated a wall with a sweep of his hand. "There will be pictures of each of you on that wall. Those will be tied in to our communications system, so that the eyes will light up when each of you calls in."

"Wow," Alan said.

Jeff indicated a trunk in the corner. "I thought we'd take the pictures today, now that Grandma has sent your uniforms."

"Uniforms?" Virgil asked.

"Yeah, what a great idea!" Scott said. "Remember when we helped at the plane crash, the emergency services people said we should have had uniforms!"

Jeff opened the trunk and pulled out a blue jumpsuit. "These are made of a special material. They won't tear, and they'll be warm or cool as needed. The material is pretty tough, but don't count on it stopping a bullet."

"Although it's s-s-supposed to be better than kevlar," Brains inserted.

"Still, don't count on it," Jeff said. "Grandma had to use a special sewing machine to make these, and special cutting tools." He looked inside and found a label. "This is yours, Scott."

Scott took it. He read the label and chuckled. "Grandma is still embroidering our names on our clothes."

Jeff distributed the other jumpsuits.

"There's one left," Gordon said as he took his.

Jeff pulled it out. His eyebrows lifted. "Seems this one is for me."

"What are those?" Alan said, seeing there were other items in the trunk.

"Oh. Each of you gets a sash. Scott's is blue, Virgil's is yellow, John's is purple, Gordon's is orange, and Alan's is white." He handed them out, then looked back in the trunk. "I guess mine is gold."

"Are you going out on missions with the rest of us?" Scott asked.

"I wasn't planning to," Jeff said. "I was going to stay here and coordinate. Maybe Grandma thought I was." He reached into the trunk again. "You all get hats, too." He held up a peaked blue cloth beret-style cap.

As Scott took and adjusted his, he said, "There's a mirror in the inside lid of the trunk. Let's see."

The brothers took turns looking at the mirror and at each other. "I think we look pretty good," Virgil said.

"Yeah," Scott agreed. "And these suits are really comfortable. I don't even notice the sash as I move around."

Brains got a digital camera and took pictures. Even Jeff put on his uniform, at the urging of his sons, and got his picture taken as well.

Back in Malaysia in his hideaway, The Hood had finished making the image of his half-brother and implanted the hairs in it. Now was the time to test it.

"Kyrano!"

Back at Tracy Villa, Kyrano paused while stocking the kitchen.

"Kyrano! You are in my power!"

Kyrano slid to the floor and rolled from side to side in pain. "No...no."

"Kyrano! Speak! Are the machines finished yet?"

"No...."

"You cannot resist me!"

"No...they have only started."

"Excellent!" He turned away, breaking the mental connection.

Back at Tracy Villa, Kyrano picked himself up off the floor. His doctor had always told him that since he had low blood pressure, he could have dizzy spells. That is what must have happened. He went back to stocking the shelves.

In Malaysia, The Hood chortled to himself. "It works. Now I have only to wait!"

10

As soon as Alan returned from Florida, Jeff set to work retraining him on the Tracy Weld. This time, with Alan's full concentration on what he was doing, he quickly learned the technique as well as his brothers had, and began helping John build the spaceship.

The first craft finished, though, was Gordon's 30-foot-long submarine. Gordon checked it, stem to stern, and Brains rechecked it. Then Brains called everyone over to paint it. "Just as I invented the alloy that we're using to c-c-construct the vehicles, I have a special paint, too." He showed them all how to apply the paint with the special sprayers; then they used lettering guides that Jeff cut on a jigsaw. Gordon became so excited that he reversed a letter and it had to be painted over and repainted. Eventually, they had "Thunderbird 4" clearly spelled out.

When finished, they stood back and admired the result. Jeff put a hand on Gordon's shoulder. "Good work, son."

Gordon turned to him. "You did half of it, Dad."

Scott rubbed his hands together. "So, don't just stand there, try it out!"

Jeff raised a hand to get their attention. "Let's settle one issue right now: only Scott and I have test pilot experience. Either he or I are going to be in each craft as we try it out. No exceptions."

Each of the brothers answered with some form of "Sure, Dad."

Jeff patted Gordon on the back. "Okay, son, let's go." He swept his hand behind him. "The rest of you stay clear."

The others stepped back as Gordon and Jeff climbed into the submarine.

"I hope you weren't thinking of driving," Gordon said as he sat in the pilot's seat and strapped in.

"You're the underwater expert," Jeff said as he secured himself in the jumpseat.

Gordon carefully checked all the control monitors.

"We're going to call this our 'emergency launch,'" Jeff said from behind him. "Normally you would be dropped in a pod from Thunderbird 2."

"F.A.B.," Gordon said.

Jeff chuckled, pleased how quickly their call sign had caught on. "Call it out."

"Monitors show clear all around. The hangar door is open, the runway is clear, the dock is set to tilt into the water. Commencing ignition." He flipped a switch and the jet engines hummed into life. "Moving forward." The submarine slowly and smoothly rolled out of the hangar and onto the runway, and gathered speed as they moved toward the dock. "Whee!"

Jeff opened his mouth to caution against getting too excited when the craft tilted downward and water splashed onto the windshield. The submarine lurched slightly then gained speed again once completely submerged. Gordon rocked the submarine from side to side.

"Gordon," Jeff said softly.

"You aren't getting seasick, are you, Dad?"

"No, but you want to take it easy the first time out."

"We gotta find out how far it will go sometime."

Brains's voice came through the craft's radio. "How's it g-g-going?"

"Smooth as silk!" Gordon said into the speaker.

"T-t-take it down as far as you can. I need to know if it will stand up to the pressure."

"F.A.B." Gordon dove at an angle because the extinct volcano, whose top was Tracy Island, had a wide base.

While they descended, Jeff kept quiet, hardly breathing, listening for the sounds of creaking or cracking. He heard nothing but the engines, however.

After a while, Gordon said, "We're at sea bottom."

"How is it?" Scott's voice asked.

"Fantastic!" Gordon checked all the instrument readings. "Everything looks great."

"Okay, c-c-ome back," Brains advised.

"F.A.B." Gordon worked the controls. The submarine did not move.

"Try it again," Jeff said.

Gordon did. Nothing happened. He turned back to Jeff. "Let me see if it will go forward."

"Okay."

Gordon had never cut the engine; it had idled as they sat there. Under Gordon's direction, the craft moved forward. Then backward. Then it turned around. But it would not go up.

Jeff unlatched the seat restraints and stood behind Gordon's chair. "Is it the ballast?"

Gordon checked the instruments. "Yeah." He flipped a switch. "This says it's releasing the ballast, but it isn't."

"You mean you're stuck down there?" Virgil's voice came over the radio.

"No," Jeff and Gordon said at the same time—Jeff firmly, Gordon calmly.

"We just have to figure it out," Gordon added casually.

"Are you in any trouble?" Scott's voice asked.

"Naw. I put that last week's worth of food Kyrano sent me at the rehab center in the food locker. We've got cots down here and a working toilet. There's plenty of stored oxygen. We could stay three to four days without a problem."

"Well, I'm planning on being home for supper!" Jeff insisted.

Gordon chuckled. "Okay, Dad." He released his seat restraints and went back to get the tool kit. "Let's do the analysis."

Jeff got the plans for the submarine and spread them on the floor. Brains did the same at the hangar. Tracing the connections, they found the main ballast system and the backup system had been cross-wired, so that neither worked. After a couple of hours, however, Jeff and Gordon had repaired the problem. They again strapped in and Gordon released the ballast controls. The submarine started to float upward. With the engine engaged, Gordon guided the submarine back to the island, up the dock, across the runway, and back to the hangar.

When Jeff and Gordon walked out of the submarine, they found the others running to them.

"It works!" Gordon announced, as his brothers shook his hand and patted him on the back.

Countdown to Action!

When the celebration had died down, Jeff said, "Let's take a lesson from this: something goes wrong on the first run of almost every craft I've ever piloted. We need to be sure we're not overconfident."

"And ch-ch-check the backup systems," Brains added.

With the submarine complete, Gordon helped Virgil with Thunderbird 2 and Jeff helped Scott with Thunderbird 1. Jeff updated the work schedule every week so that some time would be spent on the house, as well. Nonetheless, with all the Tracys and Brains working, the building went faster.

When Thunderbird 1 was complete, Jeff had each of his sons, and Brains, independently check everything from top to bottom. John caught a couple of fuel injectors and power lines which he felt were inadequate for the amount of thrust that the vehicle needed; Brains made the proper adjustments.

"Good work, John," Jeff said once they were installed.

"Building Thunderbird 3 gave me an idea of the dimensions required; Alan and I did some tests just forcing air through the intake to see what happened."

"Yeah, Alan's pretty good at that sort of testing," Scott teased, turning to his brother.

Alan threw up his hands. "I see you guys are never going to let me forget that homemade rocket I shot off in college."

"Homeland Security will never let us forget it," Jeff said. "They thought it was a terrorist attack. It was all I could do to keep you out of jail!"

"Since you bring that up, Dad," Scott said, "what's to prevent someone from thinking that Thunderbird 1 is a terrorist missile?"

"All of the aircraft have some s-s-stealth features," Brains pointed out. "They should be v-v-virtually undetectable."

"'Virtually' is the operative word," Jeff said. "They'll still be able to track us to some extent. The first public mission is going to be tricky, no doubt, but after that, the world will get used to us flying around."

"We hope," Virgil said.

Jeff turned to him. "At least we should be relatively safe for our test flights. We won't go into inhabited areas, and try to stick as close to home as possible."

* * *

Jeff took the pilot's seat in Thunderbird 1. Both Jeff and Scott wore the blue jumpsuits for protection, and both wore helmets. Each had an earpiece for communication inside and outside the craft.

"Should we have oxygen?" Scott asked as he strapped himself into the jump seat.

"That's not a bad idea, at least for the first time." Jeff put on an oxygen mask and handed another to Scott.

"The ship was designed so that you s-s-shouldn't need either a helmet or oxygen," Brains said over the radio.

"This is a test flight, Brains; anything can happen," Jeff said. He strapped himself in and grasped the levers on either side. Taking a deep breath, he said, "Okay. First we see if the conveyor belt works to get us to the launch bay."

"Uh, Dad," Scott said tentatively.

"Yes, Scott?"

"I sorta tried that on my own, down to the launch bay and back," he replied, almost apologetically, "when everyone else was asleep."

"Hm. I thought that might be too tempting," Jeff murmured.

"You don't mind?"

"Well, they used to say, 'no harm, no foul,' but I don't want you boys running the aircraft out on a joy ride."

"No, sir!"

Jeff heard his sons' voices over the radio and Scott's behind him. "Good." He took the controls in hand again. "Now let's see if I can do it, too." He pushed the lever and felt the giant craft move.

Over the radio, he heard John say, "We've moved the pool, Dad. The launch bay door is open."

"Thanks, John." He watched the instruments until the laser-guided system told him Thunderbird 1 was in the correct position. He pulled the levers and the aircraft stopped. For several seconds after that, he looked over the readouts.

"Everything okay, Dad?" Scott asked.

"Yeah. I'm just making sure we're aligned correctly. You know, if all the exhaust jets don't fire at once, or if they aren't balanced precisely, we're going to hit the bottom of the pool instead of the opening directly above us."

Countdown to Action!

"I know," Scott said calmly.

Jeff turned to Scott. "Let's do it anyway!"

"Go, Dad!"

Jeff switched on the ignition and the engines roared into life. He felt the vehicle lift off the pad. The instruments showed it cleared the pool, and once well above the island, Jeff accelerated to maximum. The G-forces pushed him into his seat. As they neared 100,000 feet, Jeff radioed back to base, "Switching to horizontal flight," and leveled out. The seat turned with him. Once they had traveled maybe 1000 miles from Tracy Island, and reached their top speed of 15,000 mph, Jeff turned the aircraft around and headed back home. Again, alignment was crucial in putting the ship back into the bay, but it all happened with pinpoint precision. Once back on the conveyor platform, he turned off the engines.

"Yay, Dad!"

Jeff heard his sons cheering over the radio.

"N-n-nothing went wrong?" Brains asked.

"No," Jeff said to his surprise.

"Sometimes that happens," Scott said. "Not often, but sometimes everything's just right."

"I guess so." Jeff took off his helmet and oxygen mask, and unstrapped himself. He turned to Scott. "Your turn, son."

"Really?" Scott said eagerly.

"You're going to be the main pilot. You need to test it out."

"Yes, sir!"

Scott's flight went as smoothly as Jeff's had. To try out the swing wings, they descended toward a deserted island, with the wings extended. Scott flew around it before folding the wings back into the rocket and ascending again. When Scott returned, he brought the ship back up on the conveyor belt while John put the pool back in place. Jeff and Scott took the turntable into the lounge, which by now had been set up as Jeff's command center, with all the required instrumentation. "Well, Brains, the ship worked just as you designed it. Congratulations."

Brains nodded, but looked at his laptop readouts, which had been taking all the readings from Thunderbird 1's instruments before, during, and after the two flights. "There's some f-f-fine tuning that we could do, but yes, the ship works as designed."

"How was it?" Virgil asked.

"It was great!" Scott said. "You should feel it."

Jeff patted Scott's back and turned to his other sons. "You all will. We need to cross-train on this equipment, remember?"

"Hooray!" Alan said, then clapped his hand on his mouth. "Sorry, Dad."

Jeff smiled. "Don't be sorry, son; I thought it was great, too!"

Scott, John, and Alan worked to complete Thunderbird 3 while Virgil, Gordon, and Brains continued to work on Thunderbird 2. Jeff was particularly anxious to get Thunderbird 3 working so that they could enable the satellite. Tracy Technologies had long since finished their part of the work, and the satellite was just floating in orbit waiting for them to come and complete the installations that International Rescue would need to become operational. On the other hand, Thunderbird 2 was essential to bringing heavy equipment to a rescue site. This was a large and complex vessel, so progress was slow. Virgil's patient and detailed manner perfectly fit the requirements of overseeing its construction. Jeff worked on whatever craft needed his attention and helped Kyrano finish Tracy Villa.

At last, John came to the Thunderbird 2 hangar to announce that Thunderbird 3 was complete, checked out, and ready for launch. They all hurried over to the rocket launch bay to admire the tall red vehicle, 287 feet high with 3 struts jutting out from the main rocket and down to each of the 3 main engines.

Jeff put his hands on his hips and looked up admiringly. "Great job, boys."

No one said anything for minutes. Finally, Scott ventured, "Who's going to take it up first, Dad?"

"Hm?" Jeff realized he had been lost in wonder, as had the others. He turned to Scott. "It's going to be you, me, and John. But first, we have to get all the equipment we need on Thunderbird 5 aboard."

Alan rubbed his hands together. "Then let's get started!"

As they walked toward the barge, where all the cargo for Thunderbird 5 had long since been set aside and labeled, Scott turned to Alan. "You're not sore that you won't get to go up first?"

Alan shook his head. "The plan is still for John and me to take turns a month at a time, isn't it? In that case, I'll be piloting it often enough. Besides, I made a promise to myself that I'm in this organization all the way...with Dad in charge."

Scott clapped Alan on the shoulder. "Good. I'm late in saying this, but I'm glad you're back."

Alan smiled. "So am I."

Once Thunderbird 3 had been loaded, Jeff insisted that all three of them had to wear spacesuits on the first flight.

"Makes sense to me," Scott said, and John nodded.

They suited up inside the rocket ship; each of them had a custom-made suit in a closet inside the vessel. John's fit his tall, slim frame as well as Jeff's and Scott's fit their more muscular frames.

Jeff went through the checklist, and added, "Make sure the pressurization matches the specs. We don't want to get the bends because the air pressure isn't right."

"I know," John said.

"Fine here," Scott said.

"Good. Brains has added enhancements so the life support system will automatically monitor the pressurization once it's set."

"I'm all for that!" Scott said.

An elevator brought them up to the control room. Jeff took the pilot's seat; Scott sat in the seat next to him. John sat in the extra seat behind them.

"Buckle up." Jeff performed all the pre-launch checks and verified that the launch bay cover had opened. "Stand by for blastoff." He flipped the ignition. "Lift off."

The engines rumbled. The noise was loud, but with the sound buffers, bearable. After a few seconds, Scott shouted, "We aren't moving!"

Jeff looked at the readouts. "We need more thrust!"

John straightened up as much as his suit and restraints would allow. "Dad! You have it on manual! Place it on automatic! Let the computer do the work!"

"Got it!" As soon as Jeff hit the control, Thunderbird 3 went up like a rock out of a slingshot. "Oof!" Jeff panted as the G force pressed him into the seat. But soon the rocket reached orbital velocity and he could move around more easily. He released the restraints. "Thanks, John. I guess I'm just used to the old days when the pilot had to do more."

John released his own restraints and stood. "The manual controls are really for when the computer isn't able to function, and won't engage if the primary computer is operating properly. You'd have to shut down the primary computer first and engage the backups."

Jeff nodded. "Yes, I remember from doing those simulations Brains put us through. As I said, I just automatically went to how I'd piloted rockets for 20 years."

"Leaving Earth's atmosphere in 10 seconds," Scott said, consulting the control panel.

Jeff leaned back and flexed his fingers. "Okay. Let's get to the space station."

The radio came to life. "Base to Thunderbird 3," Virgil's voice said.

"Loud and clear, Virgil," Jeff answered. "What is it?"

"We were a little worried when we didn't see you come out of the launch bay right after ignition. Any problems?"

"Uh...just a little mixup on the launch controls. We straightened it out." Out of the corner of his eye, Jeff saw Scott and John exchange grins.

Not long after that, the space station that was to be Thunderbird 5 came into view on the screens. Scott and John leaned forward.

"Where do we dock?" Scott asked.

Jeff put a finger on the screen. "There's a docking tube. We just insert the top part of Thunderbird 3 into it, up to the docking ring."

"Oh, so that's what it was for," John observed. "I wondered why we put a cylinder on the middle of the rocket."

"Reminds me of pushing a pencil into a pencil sharpener." Scott cleared his throat. "To put it one way."

"Yeah," Jeff said. "I know what you're thinking, but Brains insists he designed it that way because it's the most secure method of docking a ship of this design."

"Let's link up, then!" John said, excited.

Jeff chuckled. "Okay!"

Countdown to Action! 141

Once the airlock was secure, Jeff led the way into the space station. The Tracy Technologies satellite construction crew had left only dim monitor lights on. Jeff quickly found the main circuit panel and pushed the illumination to full.

"Wow!" John said, looking around. The bow-shaped control room was wide and spacious, and had a huge window set into it that gave a spectacular view of Earth.

"They did a great job," Scott said.

Jeff consulted the readouts. "Artificial gravity is working, no signs at all of air leakage...okay, boys, we can take the suits off."

Once free of the suits, they worked quickly to move the cargo from Thunderbird 3 to the space station. When they had done that, Jeff called for a halt for lunch. They found chairs in the living quarters and brought them out to the main control room so that they could see the Earth as they ate.

"I never get over how awesome the Earth looks from space," Scott said.

"I never tire of it, either," Jeff added.

"Some guys new to space just press their faces to the window and stare for hours," John observed.

Jeff caught Scott's eye and pointed to John.

"Okay, Dad, I admit it," John said. "But I'm not the only one."

"We all did at some point," Scott said.

"Now that you've looked things over," Jeff said to John, "what do you think about installing the radio equipment?"

"With Brains's modular design, it'll be fairly straightforward," John said. "But it's still an afternoon's work, even with the three of us working at it."

"Can you spare me for a brief space walk?" Jeff asked.

"Where are you going?" Scott asked.

"Well, the International Space Agency's regulations say that we have to display signs of ownership. So Brains has made up a '5' for Thunderbird 5, and I'll just install that outside."

"Will that be sufficient?" John asked.

Jeff waved at the wide viewing window. "We're going to put an 'International Rescue' sign right there. It'll be readable only from the inside, but the agency allows that, though most companies put their logo on the outside."

"I wouldn't expect too much traffic in this part of space anyway," Scott said.

"No, we're well away from the main space travel lanes," Jeff assured him. "I wouldn't expect anyone to be anywhere near here."

After they had finished lunch, they set to work. Scott and John kept an eye on Jeff on the monitors as Jeff installed the sign, but there was no trouble...and considering Jeff's decades of experience in space construction, they had not expected any. When finished, Jeff came in and helped his sons install the equipment.

It did take the better part of the afternoon, but eventually it was done. John took the controls. "Thunderbird 5 to base." There was no response at first, so John repeated, "Thunderbird 5 to base."

"Hey, John!" Alan's face appeared on the communication screen. "You should have seen it! You know the portrait on the wall? Your eyes lit up when you called just now! Then the portrait dissolved and we're seeing you talking to us live!"

"It's just t-t-technology." They heard Brains in the background.

"But impressive, just the same," Jeff said.

"Are you coming back soon?" Alan asked.

"Yes, we're finished here," Jeff said. "Tomorrow you and Scott can test it out and bring more supplies up here. After you try it, we'll let Virgil and Gordon have a turn."

"F.A.B.!" Alan exclaimed.

"I'd like to be on one of those flights, Mr. Tracy," Brains said.

"Of course. You can go any flight you want."

"Dad," John said. "I just want to test out the optics. Only take a minute."

"Go ahead," Jeff said.

"Brains," John said. "Go outside and wave at us."

"F.A.B."

John adjusted the satellite's imaging controls. He zoomed in on Tracy Villa, then the veranda. Sure enough, they could see Brains looking up, waving at them.

"Okay, Alan," John said. "Tell Brains we saw him."

Alan waved to his left. "They see you, Brains."

Countdown to Action! 143

"And we'll see you shortly," John said. "Over and out."

Once John broke the connection, Jeff said, "By the way, we have other imaging satellites covering the planet. We'll be able to see anything, anywhere, just as the military does." He gestured to the middle of the station. "One more thing...go ahead and try the telescope, John. I know you've been itching to get your hands on it."

"Yes, sir!" John sprinted to the astrodome.

Jeff and Scott followed at a more leisurely pace. They found John adjusting the controls on the giant telescope. This took a few minutes, then he looked into the eyepiece and checked the monitor. He caught their eye and pointed. "That's the Tracy Nebula."

Jeff and Scott watched the reds, blues, and greens in the cloud shifting as if it were a living thing. "Awesome, John," Scott said.

"There are entire solar systems being born there."

Jeff put a hand on John's shoulder. "I was so proud when the International Astronomical Union gave it your name."

"Thanks, Dad."

"Now, since you built the rocket, you get to fly it home."

"F.A.B.!"

John smoothly disengaged Thunderbird 3 from the docking tube, turned it around, and plotted its course back to Earth. Jeff held his breath during re-entry, but not because of John's piloting—this was always a dangerous part of space flight, and even experienced astronauts took the process seriously. But John, and Thunderbird 3, held up beautifully, and John settled the rocket back into its launch bay without a problem.

Brains made his usual post-flight check, based on the data gathered from the readouts, and made some adjustments. The next day, Jeff sent Scott, John, and Alan up. Scott piloted Thunderbird 3 to Thunderbird 5, and once there, they installed even more equipment. Then they left John there to continue installation while Scott and Alan went back to Thunderbird 3. Jeff told them that once Scott and Alan were back, Virgil and Gordon would have a turn at the controls and bring John home.

Scott took the seat next to the controls and let Alan have the pilot's seat. "Think you can handle re-entry?"

Alan smiled and flexed his fingers. "Sure! I did fine on the simulations."

"Simulations and reality can be two different things."

"I know, I know," Alan assured him.

"Call out your flight list."

Alan checked the control panel. "Thunderbird 5 airlock detached...firing retros."

Thunderbird 3 moved.

"Docking bay cleared...charting course for home."

"F.A.B." They heard Jeff's voice over the radio.

Thunderbird 3 moved toward Earth. "Setting speed and angle of approach," Alan said.

The ship jolted.

"What was that?" Alan and Scott said at the same time, facing each other. They immediately turned to the readouts.

"We need the stabilizers!" Alan said, and reached for a button, but the ship jolted again, and when he put his hand on the control board to steady himself, his finger punched another button.

"Alan!" Scott shouted.

"What's going on there?" Jeff's voice came over the intercom. "Our monitors show you're spinning out of control!"

11

Scott and Alan leaned over the control panel. "What button did you hit?" Scott asked.

"Just the exterior lighting," Alan said. "This shouldn't have happened!"

"Well, it did, and now we have to do something," Scott said.

"I'm on it," Alan said. "We just need to get the stabilizers working."

"Not necessarily...."

"Scott, I helped build this ship! I know what I'm doing!"

Jeff shouted over the intercom. "Alan, get away from the control panel and let Scott take over! Now!"

"Yes, sir," Alan said softly, and obeyed.

Scott sat in the pilot's seat.

"What's happening, Scott?" Jeff asked.

"Well, first off, I think the ship came in at such an angle and speed that we bounced off the atmosphere," Scott said. "But I was watching everything Alan did and he followed the piloting directions exactly—we should have had a typical re-entry."

"Any ideas as to what went wrong?"

"Yeah. The displays aren't right. For instance, I can see from the outside monitor that we're spinning, and I can feel the G-forces, but the piloting display doesn't register that." He took a breath. "I'm shutting the piloting computer down and going to manual."

"Can you get it under control?" Jeff said.

"Yes, I think firing the retros briefly at an angle to our direction of spin can slow us down. Let me see." He paused as he made the adjustments. "Okay, Dad, we've stopped spinning." Scott shifted his weight in the seat. "I'm going to bring it in, now."

"Can you do that without the piloting computer?" Jeff asked.

"Yeah. It's going to be seat-of-the-pants navigation, but I've done this before."

"Done what before?" Alan asked from behind him.

Scott turned briefly. "Re-entry without relying on an instrument panel. Going in by the feel of the ship."

"Okay, Scott," Jeff said over the intercom. "Keep in touch."

"Allowing for the brief communications blackout during re-entry, sure." Scott felt grateful for the array of monitors, which showed all sides of Thunderbird 3. Using those, and the manual controls, he guided the ship back into the atmosphere, and then back to Tracy Island by simple GPS.

Once they had settled into the Thunderbird 3 launch bay, and were waiting for the bay to cool enough so they could leave safely, Scott and Alan unstrapped themselves. "I know what's wrong," they said in unison.

"Then let's go," Scott added.

When they reached the computer core, they sat on the deck, took off the outer panel, and looked inside. "That's it," Alan said. "The shielding on the piloting computer slipped off."

"Brains must have forgotten to put it back when he made the adjustments after the first flight," Scott said.

Scott's wristwatch beeped. "Permission to come aboard?" Jeff asked.

"Sure, Dad. Alan and I found the problem."

"Yeah. Brains and I figured it out. We'll be right there."

While they were waiting, Alan asked Scott, "Is Brains absent-minded?"

"Not usually. But no one is perfect."

When Jeff and Brains arrived, they, too, stooped and checked the computer core. "I know I put the shield back in p-p-place," Brains said. "I know it!"

Jeff reached in and picked up a small metal piece. Bringing his hand back, he held it up for the others to see. "And you did," Jeff said. "But the supporting brackets shattered."

"That's no good," Scott said. "We have brackets of that sort throughout all of our machines."

"Are they going to start falling apart?" Alan asked nervously.

"No," Brains said. "When I put the magnetic shielding back in place, I used the b-b-brackets that came with the computer package, not the ones we used in construction."

Scott sighed in relief.

"Obviously, those sorts of brackets are fine for an office computer, but not for our purposes," Jeff said.

"I did check the s-s-specs, Mr. Tracy."

"I know, Brains," Jeff said kindly. "But when we were constructing the moon base, we found that not all of our modules were as good as the specs. We learned either to test first, or know which companies did."

"I'm sorry. I want to assure you, that I've tested e-e-everything I've built so far. This was the first time I've just relied on specs alone."

Jeff nodded. "That's why your work so far has been outstanding."

"It won't happen again, Mr. Tracy."

Jeff put a hand on his shoulder. "Everyone makes mistakes now and then. It's what we do about them that counts."

Brains gestured toward the computer motherboard. "I set those magnetic c-c-components that we sent to Thunderbird 5 right next to the outer panel. It had to have affected the computer memory and therefore the displays."

"We're lucky that the rest of the computer systems, and the backups, were still shielded," Jeff observed.

Scott looked up at Jeff. "Then the re-entry problem really wasn't Alan's fault."

Jeff put his hands on his hips. "That's not the point, Scott. The point is that Alan was too inexperienced to immediately realize that the readings weren't matching the reality." He nodded to Alan. "He'll get better the more he pilots the ship, but until he does, I'm going to have you go along with him on the missions."

"Okay," Scott said, and got to his feet.

"I'll stay and f-f-fix this, Mr. Tracy. It won't happen again."

"Thanks, Brains," Jeff said.

Alan stood and silently followed Scott and Jeff out of the ship. Eventually, they would have a system where one of the couches would take them to and from Tracy Villa by conveyor belt, but that had not yet been set up. Instead, they exited by the airlock door and took the monorail back to Tracy Villa. No one said anything on the short trip. When they got back home, Jeff walked to his study. Alan headed to his room.

Scott followed him. "Uh, Alan?"

Alan stopped and turned. "Yes, Scott?"

"You aren't going to pack and leave again, are you?"

Alan's brow furrowed. "Don't be silly. Why would I do that?"

"Well, Dad yelled at you and all when he told me to take over."

"I said I'm staying for good, and I am."

"You don't mind me having to go with you on Thunderbird 3?"

Alan grinned. "You heard what Dad said: that I'd get better the more I pilot the ship. That means he's going to let me pilot it, and pilot it a lot. That's all I care about!"

With Thunderbirds 3 and 5 in working order, all of them worked together to complete Thunderbird 2. At 250 feet long, with a wingspan of 180 feet, the beetle-shaped aircraft filled the hangar. When everything seemed to be in place, Virgil sat in the pilot's seat with everyone else standing behind him. The cockpit was illuminated by the hangar lights shining in through the windows, and the electric lanterns they all carried while building the airship. Virgil switched the cockpit lights on, while everyone else turned the lanterns off.

"Here goes nothing," Virgil said breezily, and hit the starter.

Nothing happened.

"Is it a short?" Scott said.

Virgil checked under the control panel. "Everything looks fine here."

"Try it again," Jeff said.

Virgil did. Nothing happened.

Jeff scratched his head. "Okay, boys, let's check everything again." He divided them up and assigned each a separate part of the ship. Three hours later, they came back together, each asserting he had found nothing wrong with the circuitry or connections.

Virgil settled back into the pilot's seat. "Third time's the charm." He hit the starter.

Nothing happened.

Jeff sighed explosively.

"It's g-g-gotta work!" Brains exclaimed.

"Okay, okay, we just need a rest," Jeff said. "Let's take a day or two off and get back to it later. We're probably just too close to it. We have to build a conveyor to take the crew from the house to Thunderbird 3, and we need to finish the chute to take the pilot to Thunderbird 2, and finish the passenger elevator for Thunderbird 2. We'll work on those."

"I'm sure if I just tried again, I'd find the problem," Virgil said confidently.

Jeff patted his shoulder. "And you will, but not today. We need to take a break."

Jeff had purchased two identical green couches for his study. Directly under the study, they had modified a natural fissure in the rock to use to convey the crews to Thunderbird 3. The plan was that whenever the crew was needed, a rectangle in the study's floor would sink until it reached the floor of the hangar, then go horizontally to the Thunderbird 3 launch bay, where the conveyor would then stop and rise again right into Thunderbird 3. Meanwhile, a separate hydraulic system would lift another rectangle to fill in the hole in the study floor.

The idea worked well in practice, too. Scott and Virgil anchored the couches to the floor rectangles, and the rectangles, in turn, to the steel shafts that would cause the rectangles to rise or sink. They installed the controls for the system in Jeff's desk.

Virgil wiped his hands on a rag and put the rag back into the pocket of his work coveralls. "Who wants to try it first?"

Gordon and Alan scrambled onto the couch, then playfully tried to push each other off.

"Okay, okay," Jeff said. "You can both try it!" He sat at his desk as his two sons sat up straight on the couch.

"What's going to prevent them from slipping off as it goes down?" John asked.

"There ought to be a safety bar, like on the amusement park rides," Scott said.

"There is," Brains said. "It's t-t-transparent, and will come up and over as the c-c-couch goes down."

"You put it on the couch yourself?" Virgil asked.

Brains nodded. "W-w-atch."

Jeff touched the control and the couch began to sink. John and Brains stood close to the rectangular hole. "Oh, yeah, I see it," John said.

"It's there!" Gordon called up through the hole, just as the rectangle was filled in by the other couch, which rose up through the floor.

Through the monitors at Jeff's desk, they could see the conveyor bring Gordon and Alan smoothly to Thunderbird 3. Then Jeff worked the controls again and Gordon and Alan came back.

"Whee! That was fun!" Gordon said, once safely back in the study.

Jeff ran his hand over the signed and numbered print—one of Lucy's—on a wall panel of the lounge. The original hung in his bedroom. She had painted the rocket that had taken him to the moon, depicting it during takeoff, with steam coming out of the vents. Appropriate, then, Jeff thought, that this wall panel would tilt and take one of their sons to an aircraft that would carry him to even greater tasks.

He stepped away from the wall and looked around. None of his sons was nearby. They had all gone to Thunderbird 2 to watch and see if the chute would deliver Virgil to the pilot's seat. Using his wristwatch telecom, Scott had told him it had. Jeff had heard the swish and clink of the chute resetting itself. His sons would be on the way back, but it would take a few minutes.

He pressed his lips together and faced the panel again. "Oh, what the heck," he murmured to himself. Back against the wall panel, he tapped the painting lightly. It tilted, and he was deposited upside-down into a padded lidless box. He waited for the box to swing around and send him down the chute, as it had just done for Virgil. But it did not. After about a minute of just lying there, upside-down, he noticed the wall panel had remained open. Embarrassed, he called out, "Uh...help!?"

A voice called back, "Is that you, Jeff Tracy?"

"Yes, Kyrano! Down here!"

Seconds later he saw Kyrano peering down at him. "Just a minute. I will help." He disappeared and reappeared again with a billiard cue—one of the boys must have brought one up from the game room. He extended it to Jeff, who took it and managed to climb back up and through the hole.

"Thanks, Kyrano," he said as he pushed the wall panel back into place.

"You're welcome."

Jeff leaned the cue against the wall. "Uh...don't tell the boys."

Kyrano smiled. "I will not." He indicated Jeff's desk where a tray with a coffee pot and coffee cups had been set. "I brought fresh coffee."

"Thank you."

Just at that moment, all five sons and Brains appeared. Virgil carried a tool box. "It worked great, Father, but I was almost stuck at the start. I think that I just need to check the ball bearings and maybe trim the sides of the box a little, and it'll work fine from now on."

Jeff patted him on the arm. "Good work, son."

Virgil woke suddenly in the middle of the night. He got out of bed, grabbed his robe, put on his slippers, and padded to Jeff's study. On the veranda, he saw John with his Dobsonian looking up at the stars.

John turned to him. "Midnight snack?"

"No," Virgil said softly. "I just figured out how to get Thunderbird 2 going."

"Great. Can I come with?"

"Sure."

Instead of Virgil taking the chute, they both took the newly-installed passenger elevator to Thunderbird 2. Virgil turned on the lights, led the way to the power generator, and took off the casing. He turned to John, smiling. "What do you see?"

John bent and examined it closely. "Nothing's out of place."

"Then there's no reason why it shouldn't work."

John shook his head. "No reason at all."

Virgil grinned. "Exactly." He strode across the room and motioned to John to follow. Activating the computer console, he put the circuit diagrams on that part of the ship on the screen. "See?" He put his finger on the power generator grid.

"This particular part came from one of the manufacturers Sir Jeremy ordered from."

"Right. We needed that to handle the increased power load."

"But we still had to modify it for our purposes once they got here."

"Right. I remember doing that for the Mole and Thunderbird 3."

Virgil led John back to the power generator. "Now look."

John did. "Oh! Whoever did put in this part forgot to replace the original power couplings with the enhanced power couplings."

"It couldn't channel the increased power load."

"And we didn't see it because you really have to look closely to tell ours from theirs. Because we assumed it had been changed, we assumed it looked right."

"Okay! Let's fix it."

Less than a half hour later, Virgil sat in Thunderbird 2's pilot seat, with John standing behind him. He hit the ignition. The airship's systems surged into life.

"Hooray!" John said, and clapped Virgil on the shoulder.

Virgil shut it down again. "Now I can really get some sleep. Wondering what was wrong was keeping me up at night."

John chuckled. "Me, too."

The next day, Jeff took the pilot's seat of Thunderbird 2 with Virgil, Scott, John, and Brains seated behind him—Gordon and Alan remained in the control room in Cliff House to operate the hangar doors and monitor the flight.

Jeff hit the starter. The others applauded as the ship powered up.

Jeff turned to Virgil. "And you said it was the power coupling?"

Virgil nodded. "Yup."

"Who put in that section of the power generator?" Jeff asked.

Virgil looked away from Jeff. "Uh...."

A long silence followed. The brothers and Brains looked from one to the other, but not to Jeff.

Jeff cleared his throat and scratched his forehead. "Hm. Now that I think about it, I believe it was me."

"We all make mistakes, Dad," Scott said. "It's what we do about them that counts."

Jeff saw the others trying very hard not to laugh, and did his best to remain serious himself. "Right." He turned back to the control panel. "Let's get this bird in the air."

Jeff was not ready to try out Thunderbird 2 with a pod attached, so he taxied out to the runway without one. The ramp came up, and Jeff started up the rocket engines. Thunderbird 2 lifted off smoothly. Behind him, the others cheered. Jeff took Thunderbird 2 once around the island and then brought it back to the runway. The airship smoothly turned around and backed into the hangar.

Getting out of the seat, Jeff said, "Your turn, Virgil."

Once everyone in the cockpit—except Brains—had a turn flying Thunderbird 2, Jeff called Gordon and Alan to the hangar and let Scott and John go to the control room. When Gordon and Alan had taken Thunderbird 2 for a spin, Gordon turned to Jeff. "Can we put the pod with Thunderbird 4 on and drop it into the ocean?"

"Yes, we need to try that, but I will be the one in Thunderbird 4."

"Aw, Dad...."

"You haven't been out of the rehab center so long that we can afford for you to get hurt again if it fails."

"Only half of the shock absorbers are p-p-powered, Mr. Tracy," Brains said. "The others are m-m-mechanical, and will work even if the power goes out completely. I tested them each individually myself before and after installing them. Even in the remote chance that 70 per cent of them fail, there will still be an adequate safety margin."

"I know, Brains, but since the chances aren't zero, there's still a risk. I'm trying it first. Then Gordon can try it if I don't have any trouble." Jeff left Thunderbird 2 and walked to the pod holding Thunderbird 4. He climbed into the submarine and strapped himself into the pilot's seat.

When Jeff signaled he was ready, Virgil took control of Thunderbird 2. He lifted it on its four stilts and signaled the conveyor belt to bring the pod with Thunderbird 4 under the airship. He lowered the ship and locked the pods in place. Two sets of locks secured the pod to the airship, and both indicators showed green. Virgil had the radio frequency to Thunderbird 4 open to communicate with Jeff. "Leaving the hangar, Dad."

"F.A.B."

Virgil guided Thunderbird 2 to the takeoff position. When the ramp had been raised, he engaged the rocket engines and Thunderbird 2 lifted off smoothly with the pod in place. About 20 miles from Tracy Island, Virgil reduced altitude and speed until the airship hovered above the surface. "Ready, Dad?"

"Any time, Virgil."

"F.A.B." Virgil released the first set of locks. He released the second set of locks. When the expected jolt of release did not happen, he checked his monitors. "It's still attached." He turned to Brains.

Brains stood and walked to the control panel, next to Virgil. He looked over the control panel and pointed to a button. "The safeties are still on."

Virgil grinned. "Oh, yes." He released the safeties. Thunderbird 2 rocked very slightly, and the monitors on the control panel showed that the pod had hit the ocean surface, just as it was designed to, flat bottom first. After a few seconds, when nothing came from Jeff, Virgil inquired, "Dad?"

"Can't you release the locks?" Jeff asked, sounding concerned.

Virgil and Brains exchanged a smile. "You're on the surface, Dad!"

"You're kidding! I hardly felt a thing!"

Gordon rose from his seat and leaned over the speaker. "Now will you let me try it, Dad?"

With all of the equipment built and past first-stage testing, and the house complete, they moved everything they needed off the barge. They used a deserted island nearby, also purchased by Jeff, to store their spare parts and robots. Since all International Rescue material had been carefully hidden, Jeff called for a crew from Tracy Technologies to come and guide the barge back to Hilo. They piloted Jeff's yacht to Tracy Island, and set course back to Hawaii on the barge the same day they arrived.

Jeff and the others stood on the veranda and watched the barge sink below the horizon. "What now, Dad?" Scott asked.

Countdown to Action! 155

"Thunderbird 3 is ready. We've taken it up and back to Thunderbird 5 often enough to work the bugs out. Now we need to go through a couple of simulations with the other major equipment. For instance, I thought we might have Virgil take the Mole to the island over there and do some drilling."

"The place where we stored the extra equipment?" Scott asked. "It's a small island; can it handle any more holes?"

"There's enough room there for a couple of test holes."

"But no real tunneling," Virgil said.

Jeff took a sip of the Mai Tai that Kyrano had provided him earlier. "We can't really go all out until we're ready to operate publicly."

"How will we know when that is?" Gordon asked.

"When we're familiar enough with the equipment that operating it is second nature," Jeff turned to John. "John, do you feel ready to go up to Thunderbird 5 and start listening in?"

John raised his eyebrows in surprise. "Sure!"

"What use is it to listen if we're not ready to respond?" Alan asked.

Jeff leaned over in Alan's direction. "We need to know the radio equipment is working, that it's picking up anything that could possibly be a distress call, and that the translators are giving us accurate information. Besides that, it takes practice to filter out all the static that you hear and pay attention to the important details."

"If I'm going to work up there, won't I need to practice that, too?" Alan asked.

"Yes, and you're going to start listening to reports through the equipment here...right after you and Scott take John up to Thunderbird 5."

Alan's face broke into a grin. "Yes, sir!"

Jeff, Virgil, Gordon, and Brains watched from the veranda as Thunderbird 3 rocketed into the stratosphere, a column of white vapor in its wake. When it was out of sight, Jeff put a hand on Virgil's and Gordon's shoulders. "Let's take a break, boys."

Jeff turned on the World News and sat behind his desk as Virgil took a seat at his newly-installed baby grand piano, playing as Gordon and Brains each took a book and read. About an hour later, the eyes on John's portrait lit up.

Jeff touched the control under his desk. The portrait now framed a live picture of John. "Go ahead, John."

"I'm here, Dad. Alan and Scott just backed Thunderbird 3 out of the docking tube and are heading back."

"Thanks, John."

"F.A.B." The portrait went back to the photo of John in his International Rescue uniform.

Another hour later, they heard the rumbling of Thunderbird 3 nearing the island. "Permission to approach," Alan said over the radio.

Jeff checked the radar, which showed no air or sea craft from Tracy Island to the horizon in all directions. "You're cleared to land."

"F.A.B."

Soon, Alan and Scott came up through the floor on the green couch.

"How'd everything go?" Jeff said.

"Smooth as silk," Alan said. "No problems."

"Alan handled the re-entry just fine," Scott said.

Jeff nodded. "Good work, boys. Take it easy for a while, and then you can do your post-flight checks."

"Post-flight checks?" Alan asked.

Jeff inclined his head toward Brains. "Brains, here, will no longer be personally monitoring your flights. His computer will collect the flight data for you to examine on your return. It'll be your responsibility," he swept his hand in a semi-circle, indicating all his sons, "to check the data on your respective vehicles, inspect the vehicles, and report on anything that needs repair or modification. Either you or Brains or Tin-Tin, when she returns, can work on maintenance."

"Now the real work begins, in other words," Scott said.

All the while Jeff had been talking, the World News channel continued to run. Just as Scott finished his sentence, the commentator on the television said, "Breaking News: a research sub from the University of California is trapped on the sea floor off the coast of the Philippines. Rescue boats are on the way. Details to follow." The screen showed a map with the sub's location indicated.

They all turned to the TV.

Countdown to Action! 157

"I know that area," Gordon said. "There are a lot of old fishing lines at the bottom of the ocean. It's easy for the propellers of those university subs to get tangled. And they don't have a porthole to see them before they reach them."

"What are their chances of rescue?" Virgil asked from his seat at the piano.

"Fairly good," Gordon said. "The rescue boats will probably send down lines and try to snag it and bring it up. It's too deep for conventional divers."

"How long have they got?" Brains asked.

"They probably have a couple of days worth of oxygen."

"...and they'll probably be fine," Jeff said. He turned off the TV and motioned for his sons to gather around his desk. "This is as good a time as any to review our rules of operation. First: if conventional rescue can do the job, we let them do it. We only go out if the situation is otherwise hopeless. Second: we need to keep in mind that it will take us twenty minutes to two hours to reach any danger zone. There will be a lot of disasters where if the help hasn't arrived by then, there won't be anything anyone can do. Third: there are some situations where all the advanced equipment in the world can't help, and we can't, either."

"Who determines what those situations are?" Alan asked.

Jeff took a deep breath and let it out. "I do."

Everyone kept silent for a few moments. Finally, Scott said, "Shall we call John and tell him?"

"Oh, I'm sure I'll be reminding all of you of this often. Imperfect as human beings are, and nature is, there will be no lack of work, and no lack of tough situations and equally tough decisions."

After dinner, the eyes on John's portrait lit up. Jeff put down his book and walked over to the desk to flip the switch. "Go ahead, John."

John's face wore a glum expression. "Everything's working fine, Father."

"You don't look so fine. Are you coming down with something?"

"Uh, no. I happened to pick up a distress signal."

"We know about the sub, was that it?"

"No, Dad. The science base at the South Pole...they called for help. One of the researchers got sick and his kidneys shut down. They improvised a dialysis machine, but that isn't doing the job effectively. The Air Force was called to deliver medicine and a real dialysis machine, but it's too cold for them to land, and too stormy right now even if it wasn't cold."

"They can drop a package in," Jeff said. "I did that myself when I was in the service."

"Yeah, but I'm tracking the homing beacon and the way it's going, it'll land at least a mile away. Dad, those scientists couldn't go 100 feet in that weather."

Scott walked up to Jeff. "Thunderbird 1's engines are rocket engines powered by a fusion reactor. They'll operate at any temperature."

Jeff took off his reading glasses and tossed them on the desk. He turned to Scott. "And just what do you think you could do?"

"I could go in, under the radar, use a hook, snag the package and drag it closer. The scientists must be tracking the beacon themselves. When they find it's close, they'll come out."

"...and see you?" Jeff challenged.

"No. The visibility in the area couldn't be more than, what, 20 feet?" He turned to John's portrait.

John consulted a monitor out of their view. "Even less than that, according to the meteorology report."

"It'll take them a while to suit up and come out. If I just fly by and drop it, I won't be in the area more than a few seconds, and I'll drop it out of the visibility range. They'll think the wind caught the parachute and blew it in their direction."

Jeff leaned forward and put his knuckles on his desk. "Scott, Thunderbird 1 hasn't been run out more than 5 hours altogether yet."

"Yeah, and I circumnavigated the globe."

"Yes, you did. But I still wouldn't feel sure of it until it had more flight time. What if something goes wrong?"

"I'll go get him in Thunderbird 2," Virgil said.

"Oh, great, then you'd both be lost," Gordon said.

Scott leaned forward from the other side of the desk and looked Jeff in the eye. "You wanted to put these machines to the test. Now's the time."

Jeff pressed his lips together and shook his head. He stood up straight. "No, Scott, you aren't going...."

The others in the room groaned.

12

"...until I tell you to," Jeff said.

Brains and the others looked one to the other, wondering what that meant.

Scott slowly straightened up. "Uh, okay."

Jeff turned to the portrait. "John, you keep Scott informed of the weather conditions."

"F.A.B."

He turned to Scott. "If you have any problems at all, and I mean any problems, you turn back immediately. Do you understand?"

"Yes, sir."

"You absolutely cannot be seen. Once the public knows about us, they'll start calling and expect us to come, and we don't even know if these machines can stand up under extended use yet."

"I understand, sir."

"What I said earlier notwithstanding, we're going to be tracking your every move on this one."

"Yes, sir."

Jeff put on his reading glasses again and jerked a thumb toward the lamps. "Time is of the essence. Get going."

Scott grinned. "Yes, sir!" He hurried over to the lamps and pulled on the supports. The turntable swung around, showing an identical wall and wall lamps on the other side.

Meanwhile, Jeff motioned to Brains. "Get my laptop set up to track him." He sat at his desk as Brains obeyed.

Minutes later, Thunderbird 1 rose out of its launch bay. Virgil, Gordon, and Alan stood on the veranda to watch; a hot steamy wind from the exhaust blew in their faces as it went up. Shortly after that, they heard the boom when Scott broke the sound barrier. Once the rocket vessel was out of sight, they scrambled back to Jeff's desk to watch the laptop from over his shoulder.

Countdown to Action! 161

"Thunderbird 1 to base," Scott's voice said over the radio, "changing to horizontal flight."

"Stay on your present course and speed for now."

"F.A.B."

Jeff turned to John's portrait, which was still "live." "Are you tracking Scott?"

"Yes, Dad."

"Keep an eye on him and keep him informed on the blizzard."

"F.A.B."

Jeff turned to see Virgil, Gordon, and Alan behind him. "Relax, boys, it's going to take Scott about an hour to get there."

Virgil went back to the piano. Gordon went to the stationary couch and picked up his book again. Alan took out his PDA and played a game on it.

While he and Brains kept an eye on the laptop readings, Jeff switched on the World News again. The commentator said nothing of the scientists in Antarctica, or even the sub, but he did speak live to a reporter in Nevada wearing a rain slicker.

"...that's right," the reporter said, "we've had 10 inches of rain in the last 12 hours and no sign of it stopping. The forecast is for even more rain. Round Lake right behind me is expected to overflow its banks sometime this evening. When that happens, the entire valley will be flooded."

"What about the dam?" the commentator asked.

"They're already sending through as much water as is safe," the reporter said. "With recent heavy rains, the lake was already 20 feet above flood stage before this particular rainstorm. The experts here think that the water will go over the top of the dam." The reporter turned. "They're evacuating everyone within a 100 mile radius. I'll report again when I'm out of the danger zone."

"Yes, make sure that you and your crew and everyone else is safe first," the commentator said. Then the commentator went on to other news.

"Say, Dad," Virgil said. "This is the sort of situation we'd respond to once we were in operation, right?"

"Yes, it is," Jeff conceded.

Gordon put his book down. "I have an idea. You said you wanted us to run through simulations, didn't you?"

Jeff nodded.

"So, let's think of what we would do if we were to go there."

"That's a great idea," Jeff said. "I'll keep monitoring Scott. Brains, you and Virgil and Gordon and Alan put together a plan."

Brains took his own laptop and sat on the couch with Gordon and Alan. Virgil, the larger one, stood behind, looking down. First, Brains retrieved maps from the U. S. Geological Survey, then from the Army Corps of Engineers.

The geological map showed a rugged area in the Rockies. Round Lake, which was indeed round, occupied a space high above the valley below. Mountains hemmed in the lake on all sides. To the immediate west lay a narrow ravine with steep sides. More mountains extended west and southwest. To the north, the mountains marched on toward Alaska. To the east and south, the mountains descended to a level plain. A dam had been built at the south end, providing power to the area and sending water in a controlled stream to the river valley below, where farmers grew various crops. A town of modest size stood in the valley.

"The obvious thing to do," Virgil said, "is to drill a hole in the west side and let the water descend to the ravine. There's nothing there but rocks."

"The problem with that," Alan said, "is that it would be obvious."

Virgil nodded.

"You're also going to have to be careful drilling," Gordon said. "That much water is going to carry a lot of power, and if it rushes at you, you could be a goner."

Brains brought up the information from the Army Corps of Engineers, showing a cross-section of the mountain area. "Yes, I remembered that they proposed a project, long ago, for flood control, to do s-s-something along those lines. As you can see, they were going to drill underground, following the lines of natural fissures in the strata, so that if the lake ever got above flood stage, the excess water would go to the ravine, as Virgil proposed."

"What happened?" Alan asked.

Jeff, who had been listening, spoke from his desk. "As I recall, some expert told them that a flood of that sort would only happen once every 500 years, and the government decided that the chances were so low they never funded the project."

"Oh, that was smart," Gordon said sarcastically.

"We could do it in a lot less time with the M-m-mole," Brains said. "What we'd have to do is start here," he indicated a point on the west side above the lake level on the east side, "and drill at a 45 degree angle toward the lake. Then we'd have to turn and drill a path downward toward the ravine, resurfacing about here." He pointed to a spot just above the bottom of the ravine.

Alan's brow furrowed. "How does that help us?"

Gordon put a finger on the laptop screen. "That first hole is the escape hole."

"Escape?" Alan said.

"Yes. After the Mole gets to the bottom, it will have to turn around and retrace the hole that it just dug, then past the escape hole toward the lake. Otherwise, it would have to toil up the surface again to the escape hole, and it's not r-r-really built to do that. Whoever is operating the Mole will then have to drill upwards until it's about even with the flood level."

"Why not drill through the bottom of the lake?" Alan asked.

Brains and Gordon groaned. "Much too much water pressure," Gordon said. "It's risky enough at the upper level."

"Besides, we only want w-w-water flowing through the hole when the lake is above flood stage," Brains said.

Gordon took a plastic water cup from the table. "It's the difference between drilling here," he took a pen and marked a place about a half inch downward from the rim, "and here," he marked a place at the base of the cup.

"With this plan, it will look as if the weight of the water naturally pushed into the main fissure and into the ravine," Brains said.

"What about the escape hole? Won't someone see that?" Virgil asked.

"Put a charge a few feet down that hole and s-s-set it off as you're leaving. The rocks will then cover it."

"Won't the falling rocks block the waterway?" Alan asked.

"No, no, no!" Gordon insisted. "The weight of water coming down that tunnel will sweep away any rocks that get there."

"What about the water coming up the escape hole?" Alan asked.

"Too far above the water level," Gordon said. "Water doesn't flow against the pull of gravity."

"The t-t-tricky part," Brains said, "is how close to the lake do we drill? If we drill too close, the water will sweep the Mole away, perhaps crush it, when the water weight pushes through the rock. If we're too far, the water won't flow in at all."

"Can't physics tell you how much rock has to be between the lake and the Mole before the water can break through whatever rock wall is left?" Virgil asked.

"Theoretically, yes," Brains said. "But as a practical matter, there are too many variables to account for. I can give you a rough figure, but it may come to the point where you drill until the Mole's sensors feel the water on the other side pushing the rock back at it."

"And then you might have only seconds to get out of the way!" Gordon said.

"You're not going at all under those circumstances," Jeff said from his desk. "The Mole's not fully tested. What if it gets stuck? Or worse, what if you have a power failure?"

Brains, Virgil, Gordon, and Alan looked from one to the other.

"You did a good job at analysis," Jeff said. "That's exactly how I want you boys to think when we officially start operating. But right now, they're evacuating the valley. It'll be flooded, yes, but there should be no casualties."

"Okay if we do some more calculations anyway?" Virgil asked.

"Sure, as long as they're done in the lounge here."

While the others discussed the Round Lake situation, Jeff watched on his screen as Scott piloted Thunderbird 1 across Antarctica. "I can see the cloud tops of the blizzard," he reported to Jeff. "I'm reducing velocity and height. I can't get anywhere near the base at supersonic speed; they'd definitely know I was there."

"F.A.B.," Jeff answered.

A short time later, Scott called again. "It's quite a storm. Without my radar screen, I wouldn't be able to see where I was

Countdown to Action! 165

going. I've deployed the swing wings, and am homing in on the package's beacon."

On Jeff's laptop, he could see a point of light representing Thunderbird 1 speeding toward another point of light representing the package's beacon.

"Okay, I'm right over it. Hovering the best I can in this wind. I've let down a line with a magnetic hook. It should be drawn right to it. Easy...easy...almost...drat! The wind moved it. Trying again. Easy...easy...got it!"

"Hang on to it, Scott," Jeff said.

"It's holding....I'm lifting it to within 20 feet of the station. I'm close enough that I can see the parachute with the camera. It's intact, and still attached. There's no doubt they'll think the wind caught it and dragged it to the station."

"Drop it and go!" Jeff advised.

"F.A.B." There was a long pause. "It's down. Retracting the line and the wings and accelerating...I'll make sure not to hit Mach 1 until I'm well away from here."

"Good work, Scott! See you soon!" Jeff said.

Scott was well on his way home when John called. "I've picked up the station's call to the Air Force, Dad. They got the package, and yes, they're telling them that the wind dragged it to them."

"That's a relief. Thanks, John." Jeff looked up to see Brains, Virgil, Gordon and Alan standing around the desk.

"We have a p-p-plan, Mr. Tracy," Brains said.

"Okay, let's see it."

Brains put his laptop down. He indicated the screen. "This is a three-dimensional cross-section of the a-a-area of Round Lake. You can see the fissures, and the drill path that the Army Corps of Engineers proposed."

Jeff nodded.

"The problem is about halfway down the mountainside, where there's a huge section of granite. That's where they expected the t-t-toughest drilling to be. In fact, they proposed a plan to the government where they would just drill that section and let the water naturally seep down the fissures and erode the area above it."

"The government didn't buy that, either, I take it," Jeff said.

"A-a-apparently not. They really couldn't count on the water doing that, anyway. But we could do that, just that, mind you, and it would put the Mole or its operator at minimal risk."

Just then, someone on the television news channel shouted, "I ain't leavin'!"

They turned to see the World News reporter holding a microphone to an old, grizzled man.

"I've lived here 60 some years, and I ain't leavin' for no flood!"

"But sir, if the water flows over the dam, or the dam breaks, you'll be washed away."

"I kin swim!" the man insisted. "You young fellers go on your way, but leave me be!"

The reporter turned to the camera and shrugged. "The authorities told us they're not taking anyone against their will once they've been warned, so they're not forcing him out. We're going out with them. Back to you."

Jeff turned to the laptop. "There's always one." He looked at Virgil. "All right, pack up the Mole and get ready to go. When Scott gets back, he can go with you."

"What about me?" Alan asked. "I'm willing to go."

"I'm the water expert!" Gordon insisted.

Jeff turned to them and said, softly but firmly, "You remember I said that with any craft used for the first time, either I or Scott have to go with it."

"B-b-but we've used the Mole," Brains said.

"Only for some minor excavations around here. This is a real-world situation and I need an expert on experimental craft. I know you boys want some action, and I can't blame you, but not this time."

Alan opened his mouth, took a breath, moved his eyes as if considering, and closed it again. "Okay, Dad, you're the boss."

Scott returned Thunderbird 1 to the launching bay with pinpoint precision. When he came back into the lounge, Jeff walked over to give him a hug and a pat on the back. "I'm proud of you, son."

"At least we know Thunderbird 1 can perform in a real rescue situation." Scott looked over to the couch where his brothers and Brains had gathered around Brains's laptop. "What's going on?"

Jeff explained.

Scott's eyebrows went up. "You want me to go right out again?"

"You're not tired, are you?" Jeff asked.

"No, sir! I just...didn't expect to go again so soon."

Jeff motioned. "Then take the elevator. Virgil's already in Thunderbird 2."

As Thunderbird 2 left Tracy Island, John's portrait lit up. Jeff walked over to the desk and touched the controls. "Go ahead, John."

"Remember that university sub, Dad?"

"Yes."

"Well, they radioed to the rescue ship that they're taking on water."

"Hasn't that ship snagged them yet?"

"The rescue ship says they're trying, but the sub is at the bottom, tangled in old abandoned fishing line and a bunch of other junk, and they can't grab onto it."

Gordon took a step toward Jeff's desk, turned, and strode from the room. Jeff looked up, watched him leave, and turned back to John. "Okay, thanks, John. Call if you hear anything else."

"F.A.B."

Minutes later, Gordon rushed in, laptop tucked under his arm, and stopped at Jeff's desk. He set the laptop down and put a relief map of the southern Pacific ocean floor on the screen. "Look, Dad, we're here...and the sub is there. It'll take maybe an hour to get there, two at the most. I know this area of the ocean like the back of my hand. Let me go out there."

"Aren't they going to notice Thunderbird 4?"

"Brains set up Thunderbird 4 so its sonar profile will look like a small whale. They'll think it's some sea creature nosing around."

"I know you said they don't have a porthole, but do they have a camera?"

"Dad, it's the bottom of the ocean. It's dark down there!"

"Do they have lights?"

"They're tangled in an old fishing net with a lot of junk embedded in it and moving back and forth trying to get free. They're probably in a cloud of sand and debris. They aren't going to see me."

"What will you do?"

"Just snag the line of the rescue ship and hook it onto the university sub. Take me a few minutes at the most. They'll think the hook finally caught, that's all."

Jeff looked Gordon in the eye. "You sound pretty confident."

"I am." Gordon crossed his arms in front of him.

Jeff sighed. Before Gordon could protest, he said, "Okay, use the emergency launch."

Gordon's face brightened. "Thanks, Dad!" He hurried off.

About an hour later, Kyrano walked in with a tray holding a coffee pot and fresh coffee cups. He set it on Jeff's desk, next to the two laptops. "More coffee?"

"Always!" Jeff reached for a cup, but Kyrano had already started pouring. He accepted the cup with a smile. "Thanks!"

"Where are the boys?" Kyrano asked.

"Brains and Alan went to Brains's lab to be ready to do some calculations for Thunderbirds 2 and 4 if they call in." He motioned to the laptop screens. "I'm tracking them here."

"You are worried about them?"

Jeff took another gulp of coffee. "No....well, yes. I'd planned on calmly doing some controlled simulations before going public, and here they are making tests on equipment with lives in the balance. Not exactly how I thought we'd get started."

"Life doesn't always follow a plan, Jeff Tracy."

Jeff smiled. "Don't I know it." He took another sip of coffee. "It's harder to restrain them than I thought. I guess we'll have to make the next mission the first public one, whether I like it or not...provided the equipment tests out, of course."

"It will. You and the boys have done very well."

"We couldn't have done it without you, Kyrano, and that's a fact." He raised the coffee mug as if making a toast.

Before Kyrano could respond, the eyes on Penelope's portrait lit up. Jeff flipped a switch. "Don't tell me you have a problem."

Countdown to Action! 169

Penelope appeared live on the screen. "Oh, there's no problem, Jeff. Quite the opposite. I've called to let you know that Tin-Tin arrived. We're having a marvelous time!"

Tin-Tin appeared next to Penelope. "Hi, Father!" she said, spotting Kyrano in the room.

"It is good to see you, daughter. You look lovely."

"Thank you, Father. Europe was wonderful. You should see what I bought you in Italy."

"And we're busy shopping here, too," Penelope added.

"When will you be coming home?" Kyrano asked.

"Soon, Father. Penelope says she'll refer me to her travel agent to make flight reservations."

"We'll be happy to see you back here," Jeff said.

"Speaking of there," Penelope said. "How are your preparations coming along?"

"Um...a little faster than even I expected. Scott already tested Thunderbird 1 in Antarctica. Gordon's on his way to the Philippines, and Scott and Virgil are on their way to Nevada."

"I think that's wonderful, Jeff. I can't wait until the whole world knows about International Rescue."

"To tell you the truth, I could wait a little longer!"

"But the world can't. You know that, Jeff, that's why you started International Rescue in the first place."

"Yeah, I guess watching out for the boys made me lose sight of the larger picture."

"And they'll do fine. You've raised them well."

"Thank you, Penny."

"Since the boys are on their test missions, I'll let you go. But I'm hoping to hear from you again soon."

"Okay, Penny. Good-bye."

"Good-bye, Jeff."

"Good-bye, Father. See you soon."

"Good-bye, daughter."

The portrait went back to being a photo of Penelope. Jeff turned to Kyrano. "I guess she's right. It's time to get to work."

Brains had designated a flat space about halfway up the west side of the mountains for Virgil to use as a landing spot.

He settled Thunderbird 2 on the ledge and extended the stilts to release the pod.

Scott looked at the windshield. The wipers were frantically trying to keep up with the sheets of rain. "I guess this is what we call the acid test."

"Yeah," Virgil turned to the speaker on the console. "Got those calculations for us, Brains?"

"Yes, Virgil...50 feet."

"Meaning, don't get closer to the lake bed than that."

"Right."

"Base to Thunderbird 2," Jeff said over the speaker.

"Here, Dad," Virgil said. "We've landed at the danger zone."

"How does it look?"

"Raining buckets," Virgil said. "I was about to get into the pod and drive the Mole out."

"Okay. Scott, you are to stay in Thunderbird 2 in case Virgil needs assistance. If you're both in the Mole, no one will be there to help you if you get stuck."

"F.A.B. But I'll monitor Virgil's progress from within the pod."

"That'll be fine. Good luck, and keep in touch."

"F.A.B."

Virgil climbed into the Mole. Video and radar and sonar screens showed him what was in front and behind the machine. Brains had programmed the route into the piloting computer at the base, and this showed as a red line on one of the monitors.

The Mole machine was mounted on a tractor; the rail lifted the rear of the machine to a 45 degree angle. Virgil started up the giant drill at the front; when that was spinning, he engaged the rocket engines at the rear, which drove the machine into the ground. Within seconds, the machine was completely below the surface.

First, Virgil drilled down. Then, he turned the machine into a narrow fissure and drilled parallel to the surface. The plan was to follow that to the granite formation and drill through that, and he kept to the route, but his sensors told him that water had already seeped into the fissure. "Scott?"

Countdown to Action!

"Yes, Virgil."

"There's water down here already. Can you get me Brains?"

"Right away!"

Brains came on immediately. "I'm looking at your monitors on my laptop, Virgil. I see the water registering on the sensors."

"Shall I go back or keep going?"

"I'm showing that you're making fast progress."

"Yeah. I'm right at the granite...now."

"Keep drilling."

"F.A.B."

"Your sonar shows that there's no movement of the lake bed right now. The water seeping through the fissures probably has been doing so for a c-c-couple of days. It should hold for a while longer, at least."

"I'm moving fairly quickly through the granite, too. Brains, the Mole is a great success!"

"Don't c-c-congratulate me yet. Keep an eye on the sonar. If it shows sudden movement or if you feel the ground shake or hear rumbling, bring the Mole to the surface immediately."

"F.A.B." Virgil continued to guide the Mole through the granite formation. He was almost through when the sonar beeped, alerting him to something coming in his direction.

"Virgil!" Brains shouted over the intercom.

"I see it! I'm almost through!"

"You have to go to the surface!"

"I'll get out faster if I keep going forward. There's too much granite on top of me and very little in front." He turned the rocket engines to maximum.

"Virgil! I hear rumbling!" Scott said over the intercom.

"I know! I know! I'm almost through!"

"Virgil, get out of there now!" Scott shouted.

"I'm out! Going up!"

"Hurry, Virgil!" Scott said.

"I'm out!" Virgil said. "I'm turning the Mole to climb up the mountain." No sooner had Virgil done that than water raged out of the hole he had he had just made. The exterior cameras showed the ravine behind him flooding.

Virgil heard Scott sigh over the intercom. "Good work, Virgil!"

"Thanks, Scott. It's going to be awkward getting the Mole up the mountain again; it's made more for underground travel than aboveground travel."

"I can fix that!" Scott said heartily. He got out of the pod control room and climbed into a recovery vehicle. Once outside the pod, he shot down a line with a magnetic disc at the Mole. The disc attached; he winched Virgil up the mountain. From there, Virgil was able to back it onto the tractor again, and put the tractor in the pod. Scott followed with his vehicle, and they closed the pod doors.

Scott hugged Virgil as he climbed out of the tractor. "I thought we were going to lose you."

"I was a bit worried myself." He frowned. "Shall we tell Dad?"

"Wasn't he keeping watch on his own laptop?"

"I thought so, but he didn't say anything."

After Virgil again took the pilot's seat and locked the pod into Thunderbird 2's frame, he called home. "Thunderbird 2 to base. Mission accomplished. Taking off."

"I have to tell you, Virgil," Jeff answered, "that I was holding my breath for a while there."

"So that's why you didn't say anything," Scott teased.

"I wasn't going to interrupt Brains while he was telling you how to save yourself, that's for sure!" Jeff insisted.

"Sorry, Dad," Virgil said.

"Don't be sorry. You saved at least one old man's life. We thought we had covered all the safety issues, but something unexpected came up. This won't be the last time. The important thing is that we didn't panic, we found a solution, and you're all safe. In fact, that's more important than the fact that the machines all worked above and beyond expectations. We can replace machines. We can't replace you."

"Thanks, Dad," Virgil said.

"But I want you to get back here as fast as you can. Gordon went out to rescue that university sub and we've lost communication with him."

Jeff turned to John's portrait. "Anything from Gordon, John?"

Countdown to Action!

"No, but really, Dad, I'm not particularly worried. Gordon may have had to switch to silent running to avoid detection."

"Yes, I know, but the problem is, until he checks in, we have no way of knowing if Thunderbird 4 has failed or he's just keeping a low profile."

"I'll let you know if I pick up anything."

"Thanks, John." Jeff thrummed his fingers on his desk.

"Thunderbird 2 to base. Permission to land."

Jeff swung around and checked the radar. No ships or aircraft from horizon to horizon. "Permission granted, Virgil. Come on in."

"Did you hear from Gordon?" Scott asked.

"No, we're still waiting."

"He may be okay."

"I know, Scott."

"Shall I change course and go after him?" Virgil asked.

"No, bring Thunderbird 2 in. But drop Pod 1 with the Mole and pick up Pod 4 with the track for Thunderbird 4, just in case."

"F.A.B."

When Virgil and Scott reached the lounge, Jeff walked to them and shook each of their hands. "Great work, boys. I'm proud of you. The World News is already reporting a significant drop in the water level. The Army Corps of Engineers is saying that the water poured down naturally into the fissures."

"The initial hole that Virgil drilled collapsed in on itself just before we took off," Scott said. "We didn't even have to set a charge."

"No evidence we were ever there," Virgil agreed.

Jeff nodded.

"Any news from Gordon?" Scott asked.

"Nope," Jeff said. The eyes on John's portrait lit up. "Go ahead, John."

"Father, I just picked up a radio message from the rescue vessel to the university. They say they've raised the sub and all the students and their instructor are alive and well, though wet."

Jeff smiled. "That's great news, John, thanks."

Moments later, Jeff got a call. "Mission accomplished, Dad," Gordon said. "On my way home."

"Been a while since we've heard from you, son."

"Oh, yeah. I had to go to silent running suddenly, when a U.S. Navy ship came in to assist. The rescue craft wouldn't have detected me, but the Navy ship might have."

"Good work. I want you to be able to think fast and make decisions on your own. What happened?"

"I don't think they would have caught the sub without me. There was just too much netting and debris in the way. On the other hand, they'll never know I helped them. I just nudged the hook as it was going down and then pulled back the netting so it could attach. They have no way of knowing that it wasn't natural deep ocean currents that caused the hook—or the net—to sway."

"...or a friendly small whale," Alan added with a smile.

"That, too!"

Jeff chuckled. "Okay, come on home!"

"F.A.B."

Meanwhile, in the wilds of Malaysia, in his isolated retreat, the Hood also watched the World News, courtesy of a huge television satellite dish.

"Hm," he murmured to himself, "a lake about to overflow suddenly doesn't, a submarine in trouble is suddenly rescued, a package for a science station suddenly is blown in just the right direction. The television fools think this is just good fortune. But I have seen enough secret tests of new weapons technology to know when something is a coincidence and when it is not!" He looked over at the image he made of Kyrano. "Soon, my half-brother, we shall be in touch. Then I will know if International Rescue is ready for action!"

The next day, Jeff asked everyone there to come to the lounge. He sat on his desk, facing his sons, Brains, and Kyrano, all of whom had taken seats on chairs or the couch. John was live on his portrait; Penelope was live on hers, with Tin-Tin next to her.

Jeff nodded to Brains. "Brains, here, has finished his analysis of our impromptu 'field tests,' and he thinks that the

Countdown to Action! 175

machines are ready for regular use. I agree. Our next mission will be public."

The Tracy brothers cheered; the four brothers in the lounge slapped Brains on the back.

"That's wonderful, Jeff," Penelope said.

"I understand why you're excited. But before we find ourselves in the public eye, I just want to remind you one more time what all this means." He paused, and looking around, saw he had their attention. "First, when you go out, you'll be in uniform." He turned to John's portrait. "That means you, too, John."

"F.A.B."

"But Dad," Alan said, "no one but us is going to see who's in the space station. What does it matter how we're dressed there?"

"Professionals wear professional dress," Jeff said firmly. "And we're going to be professionals through and through, whether anyone's eye is on us or not."

Scott turned to Alan. "Remember the plane crash, when we weren't taken seriously because we were civilians? A uniform says to the world that we're trained, ready, and part of a team."

"Right, Scott," Jeff said. "And once we start, there's no going back. The world will expect us to be on call 24/7. We can't give this less than 100%. This is your last chance to back out if you have any doubts at all. Nothing will be said. All that I would ask is that you keep our secrets."

The brothers looked from one to the other.

Alan crossed his arms in front of him. "You'd have to use a bulldozer to remove me."

The others chucked. "I think it's safe to say we're all in this for the duration," Scott said, and the other brothers murmured agreement.

Jeff let out a breath and smiled. "Good." He turned to Penelope's portrait. "You're on call, too, Penny."

"Parker and I are at your service, Jeff."

"I'm packing now," Tin-Tin added. "I should be there in a day or two."

"We'll be glad to see you again, Tin-Tin," Jeff said.

Kyrano smiled. "I cannot wait to see you again, daughter."

"And I can't wait to see you, Father...and everyone else there."

"I presume you were responsible for the miraculous events of the past couple of days?" Penelope said.

Jeff scratched behind an ear. "Yeah, that was us."

"I think you did a great job," Penelope said. "I think that once the world knows about you, they'll look back and realize what you did."

Jeff sighed. "Well, I think we can live with that." He slapped his knee. "Are we ready, then?"

The others nodded and chimed in. "Yes." "Sure." "Absolutely!"

Jeff jumped down from the desk. "Then our countdown to action begins now!"